T0113313

ADVENTURES
in
THROGWOTTUM
GLEN

Wonkus

B R I A N   T .   G I L L

authorHOUSE®

AuthorHouse™
1663 Liberty Drive
Bloomington, IN 47403
www.authorhouse.com
Phone: 1 (800) 839-8640

Interior Graphics/Art Credit: Molly Alicki Corriveau

Published by AuthorHouse 12/10/2015

ISBN: 978-1-5049-4963-7 (sc)
ISBN: 978-1-5049-4962-0 (e)

Library of Congress Control Number: 2015915098

Print information available on the last page.

This book is printed on acid-free paper.

DEDICATION

....

This book is dedicated to Anton, my original storytelling audience of one, to Maxim, for later enriching the plot, to Alyona, for enduring my long second childhood during development of the manuscript, and my parents, for motivating me to bring "Throgwottum Glen" to print.

Special recognition is due to Mitch and Annette, who guided me to the moral imagination of Russell Kirk, and to "the rising generation."

CONTENTS

CHAPTER 1

A not Altogether Usual Spring Morning

*on which we meet many greater and lesser
denizens of Wiggiwump Village,
often by way of intrusions, and several events of future consequence
are passed over as trifles or overlooked entirely*

For most residents of Throgwottum Glen the day was to start calmly. Gentle and muted, the first rays of the rising sun had just peaked around the southern face of distant Tryg Massif and into the outlying marshlands. Thence they crept slowly over ancient ruins and tumbledown walls, where bygone whispers lingered in the winds. Onward, gathering purpose, they marched through the rolling hills, down into the river valley, across Cobble Bridge, along the shops lining Founders Row, and finally into the town square. In the very center, atop Spiral Tower, a watchman eagerly awaited the arrival of dawn. When darkness at last receded he hoisted a bright yellow flag.

And what happened next was a sight to behold! On the summit of the western brackawack fields two keepers would lift a sluice gate, freeing the current of the Upper Throg River. The impatient waters, swelled with melted snow from the frosty north, rushed first into a large weighted tub, which tipped into three troughs and then sprang back for the next filling. Those channels fed into still more chutes that ambled through the brackawack bushes, dripping just the right amount onto each. Finally, after cascading to the bottom of the terraced slopes the stream set in motion a set of padded hammers. One by one each pounded a tin gong, calling smartly dressed Wiggiwumps out of their dome-like houses with a gentle melody before jetting high in the air.

The Musical Fountain was the work of none other than Apseron and Lilliwan Sygard. It is hardly a secret that Apseron, a brilliant inventor (some of the time, if only accidentally) designed the silvery irrigation network. Nor is it a mystery that Lilliwan, a gifted musician (nearly always, and conscientiously so) composed the song that stirred the villagers from their sleep.

Less known is the tale of how their precocious twins, Kedra and Fruku, saved Throgwottum Glen from a looming danger. If not for their bravery, witnessed only by a Lion-Hearted Shrew and a Chattiwog, neither Spiral Tower nor the brackawack fields – indeed, hardly a single Wiggiwump home – would be left standing. In the pages ahead we shall try to render their heroic deed faithfully. But we must come to it in due course, for, as our story begins little set them apart from other 12-year olds. Or so it might have seemed, anyway.

Each had quirks, to be sure. When the weather allowed Kedra would gaze at the stars, joining them into fanciful constellations, to the derision of friends who found such pursuits hopelessly impractical. But she still took an interest in dolls, even if she pretended otherwise, and both playing with figurines and pretending not to were quite normal at her age. And she might wear her mahogany tresses in braids one day and loose the next, as any girl is wont to do. Thus, in the main, she passed as typical. For his part Fruku enjoyed watching "Captain Luminous," an old serial consigned to reruns, for which he suffered a good deal of mocking. Otherwise, like most any boy in Throgwottum Glen he climbed jinjibar trees, tracked dirt into the house, and often forgot to pat down his spiky blond hair. Thus, too, could he be taken as ordinary. On the whole the twins were respectful, well-mannered children with mild rebellious streaks; there wasn't anything uncommon in that.

On this drowsy morn, as they finished dreaming of adventures (perhaps still believing that adventures were only the stuff of dreams), GubuGar sniffed through the cracked-open door of the Sygard hut. The nose in question was attached to Gar, to be more exact, Gubu having an eye but lacking a snout. Their two necks joined into a ponderous body that waddled precariously, both because the four webbed feet were far too tiny for the load they carried and due to confusion over where, precisely, those feet should be pointed. So it was that once, near a pile of garbage Gubu pulled to the right when Gar stepped to the left, the legs became crossed, and with a loud *phwaaht* the single nose landed in a heap of rotten eggs. "Foo," squeaked Gar, the falsetto of the duo, "this stench is unbearable. And for the hundredth time, stop leading me into ruination!" "I don't smell a thing," protested Gubu in his baritone voice, "and anyway you should let me do the seeing for both of us!"

In short, the unfortunate pair of heads bickered constantly. There was one unity of purpose, however, and that was the joy of spreading their recurrent misery. On this particular morning GubuGar had been restless, and determined not to wait for the Musical Fountain before seeking sympathy. Hence with a loud *hruckk nrongg shwutt* Gar's nose poked expectantly into the Sygard household, hoping for the sweet aroma of tea. "Well?" asked Gubu. "Hrumph," answered Gar, "nothing. Have a look for yourself." The snout then withdrew, replaced by an eager

4

eyeball rolling slowly to the left and the right. "Well, you're right for a change," scoffed Gubu. "Lilliwan?"

The entreaty was drowned out by the thunderous snoring of Jax the Jiparix. In fact Jax, meant to be a guard Jiparix, should have intercepted GubuGar long before the front gate. But being an animal of great self-importance he considered such tasks as beneath him. Moreover, he was daydreaming of a good tummy scratch, which was hardly worth interrupting merely for the *shloop shlap shlup* of GubuGars' dragging extremities. And so he simply lazed on his designated rug, with fuzzy limbs spread akimbo and his long, pink tongue hanging shamelessly to one side.

"Lilliwan," repeated Gubu, this time much louder and with aristocratic airs, "have you a snack for esteemed guests?"

The intrusion might have passed uneventfully if not for the fact that Apseron, toiling through a sleepless night, had reached a defining moment. "Maybe," he would think out loud, "the purple wire ought to go here, the green there, and the gold round to – yes, that's it." "No," he would suddenly correct himself, "the green and gold must feed into the orange, which runs to . . . that's most certainly the right combination! Or," he might then backtrack, "it all beings with the . . ."

Thus had dusk passed into dawn with Apseron, sometimes hovering in place, often pacing, all the while feeling maddeningly close to an elusive goal. At last when he was finally convinced of a breakthrough, the shrill voice of Gar shattered his frail concentration. *Oh confound it,* he thought, *I was on the verge. What's this, then?* Apseron hastily put down a peculiar rod and opened the door to his laboratory. To his surprise, light flooded the room, blurring his vision. The acrid scent allowed no time for slow adjustment. "To what do I owe this honor?" he asked.

"We couldn't sleep," grumbled the Gar head, "what with all the blurpogs blurping." The said creatures were shared tenants of the boggy lowlands, known for their oily, elastic skins and, during the spring, incessant croaking. No larger than a fist at rest, while blurping the swamp dwellers ballooned three times in size, blaring sounds to match. Their sole redeeming quality, if it could be called as such, was their inability to outlive the next autumn.

GubuGar had spent the early hours trying, in vain, to cover four ears with only two front flippers. Nor could they rid themselves of the pests – whichever they slapped at would disappear only momentarily, joined in concert by a half dozen or more. "The noise this time of year is positively insufferable," Gar continued.

"He means, we are patrolling, naturally," corrected Gubu, stiffening his neck to emphasize the seriousness of this task.

"Patrolling? For what, exactly?"

"For whatever isn't here," answered Gar. "We can only declare the village safe when we don't find anything troublesome."

"You mean to say," Apseron demanded, "that you left a place where there *is* a nuisance in order to find peace and quiet. Shouldn't it be the other way around?"

"That's highly indecent of you, to suggest we should suffer like that!" protested Gubu.

"Suffering isn't in our job description," Gar added indignantly.

By this point Apseron's patience started to wear thin. "Now listen, you don't have a job description because, in fact, you don't have a job. And I don't care for you to appoint yourselves to one, particularly if that means tracking muck into my house. Shouldn't you better go patrol somewhere else?"

Gubu was unmoved. "Not before we finish our assessment."

"Assessment?"

"Must we repeat: that there is no cause for concern here," suggested Gar. "Such as, for example, no leaky roof, no blurpogs . . ."

"And," Gubu interjected, "certainly no shortage of brackawack tea. Of course for that we shall require a sample."

"A sample!?" Apseron cried. Why, there was no limit to the effrontery.

But GubuGar supposed that Apseron had not understood their polite request. "Otherwise, how can we confirm that no one pinched it," offered the Gar head.

"Again, to be clear," Apseron said, having slightly regained his composure, "in order to be certain that no one made off with my tea during the night, you propose, out of the kindness of your hearts, to drink it all yourselves."

"Exactly" said GubuGar together, pleased that their point might finally be coming across.

"Then tell me, how is that better than thievery?"

"What's strange about it?" Gar inquired. "How else can we make a clean write-up?"

"And anyway," continued Gubu "all of this not finding danger has worked up an appetite. We patrollers need refreshment!"

Apseron simply stared, silently.

"You wouldn't want to be named as uncooperative, would you?" By now the Gar head sensed the futility of their plan, but made one last effort.

"That would be quite a sight, your flippers gripping a pencil! Now, for the last time, off you go."

"We'd like to be going," said Gar.

"Except," continued Gubu, "slightly less than we would prefer to stay."

"Out!"

"Ptoo," boomed Gubu, "that's no way to treat the Factotum of the Glen!" "Come, Gubu," said Gar, similarly offended, "let us take our leave." Then the plump body grudgingly turned around and waddled off.

"It's all your fault," shrieked Gar as they passed the gate.

"Nonsense," thundered Gubu, "I told you that it was a waste of time."

At last, when the bickering could no longer be heard, the jiparix rose to his feet and bellowed a protective *oow-ooooh-errr*!

~~

In their rooms on the upper floor, the mother and children had abandoned hope of further rest. "Apseron, is everything alright?" came the gentle voice of Lilliwan from above.

"Nothing to worry about. Stay in bed," Apseron shouted back. But by then Lilliwan was descending the stairs, followed closely behind by the twins, each rubbing sleepy eyes. "What happened?"

"We had a visitor," Apseron answered, pointing to the trail of mud on the floor.

"I see." Lilliwan cast a disapproving stare at Jax, who had by then returned to his warm spot on the carpet. "Goodness, Apseron, have you been up all night?"

"Right!" exclaimed Apseron, not so much replying to the question as taking it for a prompt. "Let me show you something. Just a minute!" He darted back into his lab, from which emanated various scraping and rustling sounds. Then he wheeled out a cart, over which a sheet was draped.

"What's that underneath?" asked Kedra.

"Lurdite," Apseron proudly announced, referring to the rock mined for the building blocks of Wiggiwump houses. "But not ordinary lurdite. Watch how it . . ." he proclaimed, removing the cover.

The others stood with blank expressions. "It seems ordinary to me, dear," Lilliwan ventured. "How should it be different?"

"It should be glowing by now," Apseron replied dejectedly.

The others stared silently at the heap, blinking slowly. "Why on earth would lurdite glow?" Lilliwan wanted to know.

"Because, because," he stammered. "Well, because maybe it can!"

Lilliwan tried to be supportive. "That could be useful, I suppose."

"Another flop," sighed Fruku, not yet alert enough to choose his words carefully. To his credit, he occasionally salvaged the apparent failures. Most recently when his father's attempt at a rubber buoy shrank to the size of an egg, Fruku appropriated it as his favorite toy, an "oddball" that bounced unpredictably

"How many times must I explain – there is no such thing," Apseron insisted. "There are only successes, and ideas that are ahead of their time."

"On the scale of successful to less so, where would this one be?" Fruku wondered.

"Ahead of its time," admitted Apseron.

"I think you have invented something, Dad," Kedra offered.

"What's that?"

"A new way to say *flop*," she laughed.

"But it has to work!" Apseron persisted. "No doubt I simply need to . . ." As often occurred the sentence trailed off into a fragment.

"I'm sure you'll get it right," Lilliwan offered. Then she thoughtfully changed the subject. "What did GubuGar want this time?"

"Brackawack tea, I think."

"That's not a bad idea, as long as everyone is up. Kedra, can you put the kettle on? And Fruku, would you mind bringing a mop? Let's clean up this mess."

But putting the house into order would need to wait, for just then sharp cries pierced the air. They were faint at first, growing gradually louder until there was no mistaking the approach of the screechiwogs. As to their description, we might start by picturing the most elegant of birds, sleek, firm of purpose, and graceful of motion. If we can then imagine the exact opposite, we would approximate a screechiwog.

To start, their plump frames hardly inspired a look of airworthiness. Then came the matter of their downy feathers, which flared out in flight, creating the profile of a sideways umbrella. And we cannot fail to mention the long bent beaks, through which the most excruciatingly cacophonous of shrieks peeled. As might be supposed, it was this unfortunate characteristic that gave rise to their name.

Yet none of these peculiar features was the most distinguishing. No, what best (or worst) defined a screechiwog was its manner of flight – which is to say, backwards. There was no sound explanation for why it should be so, but for as long as anyone could remember that is how they fluttered, hind-first with their eyes facing toward the past. Thus could a screechiwog be unpleasantly surprised that its tail feathers felt cold and wet when the sky behind was perfectly clear.

The Cluster, as it was known, likewise navigated by guesswork. The backwards fliers at the front of the wedge (which could easily mutate into an arc, squiggle, or freeform configuration) would periodically bleat out a cry that meant "so far, so good." Trailing behind, the Omega Screechiwog would do its best to follow the trajectory. Should the leaders (if such term can be applied to them) crash into an object they would bellow an ear-splitting warning.

And these awful sounds, which no one should wish on his worst enemy, carry us into the second interruption of the still young day. Lilliwan, having a musical ear, instantly recognized the forewarnings of the spring migration and wisely beckoned Apseron to close the door. But being a scientist to the core he wanted to observe the phenomenon from up close. "This is exceptional," he declared. "I've never seen this pattern before!"

"Mom," Kedra asked as Apseron barely ducked a screechiwog straying from the Cluster, "will papa be alright?"

"Probably," Lilliwan replied calmly. "Maybe some sense will be knocked into him."

By then the first screechiwog had crashed into a jinjibar, emitting a loud *rehash!* followed by an *eerrff!* before, on the third attempt, finding a clear path to the next obstruction. Others careened into the ground, trees, and even other members of the Cluster. In the neighborhood it sounded as if a hundred bagpipes had been thrown on the floor and, for good measure, stomped upon by a heard of dray mules.

When by trial and error the Cluster had cleared the various obstacles and signaled accordingly, the Omega Screechiwog calibrated its path. Misjudging ever so slightly, it smacked into the roof of Mr. Makiloyd, leaving a wet imprint and bellowing a rowdy *BREEOOWWW!* It too left, squawking in the general direction of the Sygards while flying away clumsily in reverse. As the blaring faded to tolerable levels the homeowner emerged to survey the damage.

Mr. Makiloyd was a man of few words. Except, thought Fruku, when it came to lecturing the twins for letting the oddball bounce onto his yard (which, to be fair, happened from time to time) or Jax wander on his grass (which might have occurred once, as far-fetched as the idea now seemed). Fruku couldn't help but smile at the thought of their neighbor suffering the only direct hit by a screechiwog. But Mr. Makiloyd simply noted the mark on his house without concern, giving little cause for the boy to rejoice.

No sooner had the feathers settled to the ground when Mayor Tuggles appeared. As usual he was accompanied by his nephew, Humberbred, who muttered "thassamosintretingpatturn" or something to that effect. "Hm," replied the mayor, framing the wet spot with his fingers and thumbs set at 90-degree angles, "you might be on to something there. Let me mull that over. Oh, Apseron, being caught up in my thoughts I hadn't noticed you. Good morning."

"Good morning," Apseron returned. "Hello, Humberbred."

"Blezidday toya," mumbled the boy.

"Well put, indeed!" exclaimed the uncle proudly. He was the only Wiggiwump who could understand Humberbred, and somehow divined lucidity in his comments.

Satisfied that the danger had passed, the remaining members of the Sygard family emerged from the home. "Good morning to you both," Lilliwan greeted the mayor and his nephew.

"Yes, I think we can safely declare it to be," Mayor Tuggles replied, "now that the screechiwogs have passed beyond the village. Disruptive creatures, they! I don't suppose we can outlaw them?"

"Hardly," Apserson replied.

"Yes, that's also my position," Mayor Tuggles agreed. "It's a pity, though."

"You're out early," Lilliwan offered.

The mayor then made a reflective face, or what he hoped could be taken for one. "Yes," he confirmed, "I do my best thinking in the wee hours. The cool air is . . ."

"Shmulatin," Humberbred offered.

"Exactly right," the mayor continued, "stimulating. Speaking of fresh ideas, Lilliwan, it's good that I ran into you. Humberbred and I have been planning Harvest Fest. This year I really want to make it one for the ages! On that note . . . ."

But Lilliwan was spared. "Say, is that smoke?" Apseron asked, pointing to the summit of Tryg Mountain.

"Only clouds, no doubt," the mayor answered, squinting into the bright sun. Humberbred then uttered something or other that was taken as affirmation of his uncle's assessment, and the two momentarily forgot their reason for calling on the town musician.

∽〜∾

Unbeknownst, as the small crowd dispersed something amazing happened: the lurdite lit up, faintly at first, and then brightly. Jax, alone in the house, paid no attention to the strange pulsing. He had earlier ventured into the laboratory, but instead took interest in a stick-shaped instrument lying on the counter. The taste was not to his liking, and so he spat it out under the couch and fell back into a deep sleep. We will learn, in the coming chapters, how such a seemingly innocent act can have profound consequences, as well as why one single "Hm" from the mayor may set in motion a series of comedic events.

CHAPTER 2

More (and Less) than Meets the Eye

*during which we learn more about Throgwottum Glen,
the twins receive an odd diagnosis, and a random bounce
of the oddball leads to the first improbable encounter*

L
ater that week the last of the screechiwog feathers had been raked up, save for one or two that would disappear of their own accord. So, too, GubuGars' trail was washed away. As the river current diverted through the brackawack fields, the bright morning light reflected onto a marvelous riot of colors, for the flowers – orange, pink, and yellow – were in full bloom. In short, spring, in all its splendor, had arrived.

Carefree and in rhythm with the season, the villagers would awake to the soothing gong of the Musical Fountain. In turn the streets were soon to fill with the bustling of business and commonplace activity, from the opening of shops, to the unmistakable churning of pede trams, to children skipping rope. Those with time to pass would take up seats to witness the town come alive, debating this or that or watching in silent contemplation.

Let us, in the meanwhile, say a few words about the Wiggiwumps. And to do justice to their patrimony we should begin with the sundry terrain that shaped them. Orienting as Wiggiwumps do we begin in the mountainous north, whence the crystalline headwaters of the Throg fed into the valley. Much of the snow had disappeared, to return as rain over the verdant surface or filtering down into the aquifers supplying the countless wells. But the peaks remained capped throughout the year, carrying cool air into the river valley.

Trails to the east led to the Near Beyond, meandering through rich, open farm fields. Continuing on they ran into the Enchanted Forest, where the thick crown of old-growth knotty jinjibars blotted out the light and, some still feared, provided cover for sprites. Southward the groves faded into rocky Gronk Narrows, a harrowing, barren gulch best visited by day. Thence onward to the east towered the Tryg Massif, about which we may have more to add as our story unfolds.

A great expanse of sea bounded the greater Glen on the south. In the autumn the screechiwogs flew this way to warmer climes, looking, in their peculiar manner, to the territory they were leaving behind. The coast carried around to the western lowlands where the blurping had by now died down. It is here that the first settlers arrived, pressing inward.

Cobble Bridge spanned the banks where they first forded the Lower Throg many centuries ago. On the same spot a wooden crossing, hewn from local timbers, had been swept downstream before their children erected a stone replacement. Each generation in turn contributed to securing the borders, taming the land, channeling the waters, cultivating the fields, extracting riches from below the ground, and adding to the village that grew on either shore.

And what a town they built over time! First came a chapel, mills, and a market, and later guilds, smithies, a mint, schools, libraries, and a small planetarium. Makeshift log buildings gave way, one by one, to thick-walled structures of precisely cut square and arched lurdite blocks, set deep in the earth and rising several stories above. Soon the village was a center of thriving commerce and science, attracting traders, artisans, and craftsmen (as well as, we should note, the occasional unsavory character). Each left his or her mark, whether in stone or print.

Thus in the Glen, as Fruku and Kedra were born into it, nearly everything up, down, forward, backward, left, and right was so thoroughly measured, weighed, calculated, analyzed, catalogued, inventoried, regulated, and rationalized that one could (if one were so inclined) take order as a given. Many recalled the hard work that had built up this life of comfort and acted as custodians of their inheritance. But a good many squandered the gift of their leisure time. While past generations of Wiggiwumps could hardly abide the sight of cracks in the sidewalks, their heirs might regard them as trivialities, or, being caught up in philosophy, not notice them at all. In consequence the village, though retaining its stateliness, exhibited a few weeds and occasional peeling paint. Likewise, while modern Wiggiwumps dressed smartly – boots, long coats, and hats for the men and skirts and scarves for the ladies remained in fashion – the standards were slowly but surely relaxed.

These early stages of decline extended to the realms of spiritualism and the intellect. A diminishing number could recite the nuanced odes to the twilight left by troubadours of yore. In reflection one Wiggiwump might still say, "Look at the sunset – it's as if the sky were painted with heaven's own brushes!" Another, lacking interest or richness of language could answer, "Maybe so, I hadn't noticed."

And a few shunned their rich heritage in favor of bold ideals and aesthetics. Nowhere was the contrast of old and new more apparent than in the town square. To the north a medieval belfry stood, the clock on its southern face still marking perfect time. On the east rose Spiral Tower, the modern city hall. At that very moment two elders sat on a bench, discussing the merits of the design. "It resembles a corkscrew," said the first. "That is only fitting," replied the second, "as the architect certainly must have been drunk." "Not so," insisted the first, "it represents the forward march of history." In short, a novel worldview was forming around precepts not always discerned through logic, understood only to a select number, and challenged by few.

And this jumbled state of affairs brings us to the cause of the twins' troubles. In accordance with their rearing they were well-mannered children who showed a healthy respect for the rules. But there was one expectation that made them bristle, and that was *sameness*. Now, most every child wants to be accepted, and to a certain extent that means blending in with the crowd. The sort of sameness that drove Kedra and Fruku mad was different altogether, and that was enforced uniformity of thought.

For example, there was the recent botany lesson with Mr. Mramsee. "Class," he asked, holding up a picture of a tree, "Who can tell me what this is?" *Why, any four-year old could spot a knotty jinjibar,* Fruku thought. *What is the fun in that?* He whispered something to his sister. And then, as if by itself, her hand raised. "Yes, Kedra," called Mr. Mramsee, expecting a textbook reply. "The home of an enchanted forest spirit," she offered. The teacher, having a more restrictive sense of humor, sent a note home to the parents. "What use is school," Fruku asked on their walk home, "if we can't enliven the discussion?" For her part, Kedra maintained the poetic truth of her answer.

Little did Lilliwan know, as she made the rounds inside the home, that the day would hold more challenges for the twins. "Wake up," she beckoned.

"Is it morning already?" Kedra asked, rubbing her eyes.

"For some time," replied Lilliwan, throwing open the drapes. Fruku was next in line, and no more ready to leave the bed. "Rise and shine," Lilliwan called, similarly letting the sun into the room.

"Hrmmphh," Fruku groaned.

They again stayed up late talking, realized Lilliwan. *I wonder what about now.* "Let's get moving," she added. "Your essays are due." At that Kedra and Fruku snapped to attention. For their class assignment each student was asked to imagine that he or she boarded a pede tram, so called because the conjoined round wagons resembled a centipede, only to find that it went somewhere unexpected. The twins each had great hopes of taking first prize, as they excelled at creative writing and put great effort into describing the amazing journeys upon which they might embark. Thus on this day

they ran down for breakfast, and soon were bundled off to
school, buoyant for the day ahead.

Shortly after wishing them luck Lilliwan picked up
her bariharp, a traditional Wiggiwump instrument that
yielded different pitches when stretched. Her fingers glided

effortlessly over the strings, and she stopped only to revise the notes on paper. When the composition was nearly to her liking she heard her name. "You're not even fit for a speed bump," she reprimanded Jax, who in dereliction of duty felt not the slightest pang of guilt.

"Pardon?"

"That wasn't meant for you," she said, recognizing the voice. "Come in."

"Good morning, Lilliwan." The familiar face of the mayor poked through the open door. "Do you have a few minutes?"

"Well, yes, I suppose so," she replied politely.

"By the way, that piece was lovely. How is it called?"

"Thank you, Gapron. I've been working on a symphony to the forces of nature. It doesn't have a title as of yet."

"Not a problem," replied the mayor. "I'm sure we can come up with something."

Lilliwan wasn't sure how to respond to this idea, or to the next. "I wanted to return to our conversation," began Mayor Tuggles, "which we didn't quite finish last week. Blast those screechiwogs! I have a mind to fine them."

"You would have considerable support for that, no doubt," offered Lilliwan. "But easier said than done."

"My sentiment exactly," the mayor suddenly agreed. "Now, to come to the essence, I was hoping that you will conduct the brass band this year."

"Well," Lilliwan demurred, "unfortunately I am quite busy . . . ."

"That's splendid!" he replied, having taken her acceptance as a foregone conclusion. "Rehearsals start in the next week. I'll tell Ms. Brumps to contact you with the schedule." Mayor Tuggles promptly excused himself, before Lilliwan could object. The unsettling feeling lingered, and, perhaps, colored her understanding of subsequent events.

Toward the end of the school day Lilliwan received another visit, this time by her sister, Vreena. The twins adored their aunt, who taught them the best affronts and entertained with stories of their mother's childhood. Nearly every tale earned a disapproving stare from the older sister, who from a young age channeled her energy into productive pursuits (though if truth be told, had forgotten her own rebellious streak). Vreena was the late bloomer of the two. Fully mischievous in her youth, she only later discovered her passion, for literature. Vreena owned the Glen's best bookstore and took great satisfaction in her collection of old and rare materials. But she was still a bit wild at heart.

"Hello, kids!" Vreena greeted the twins as they returned. To her surprise they didn't rush to meet her. "Why the long faces?"

"It's unfair!" Kedra protested. She was visibly wound up, and, Vreena sensed, had been venting for the entire walk home.

"Did the competition not go well?" Lilliwan asked.

"Not entirely," answered Fruku. In his essay he had imagined the pede rails rising into the sky, leading on a fantastic flight through the clouds. "Kedra took third place, though."

"That's excellent," Vreena complimented her. "What did you submit?"

"I wrote about a wagon that turns into a magical carriage, which travels to a fairyland," she replied.

"You should be proud of yourself," Vreena assured. "Why the disappointment?"

"Because," Fruku explained, "the other prizes were for complete rubbish! Do you know what Humberbred managed? He simply wrote, 'I would tell the driver, Hey, stop and let me off.' And that was good enough for second!"

"And," continued Kedra with visible exasperation, "Druzina took first."

Druzina – the very name irritated Kedra – was the class know-it-all. She was flawless, completely and utterly in every way. At least she thoroughly believed herself to be, because from an early age everyone had told her so. When other infants were already managing proper speech, Druzina would have her puffy cheek (which was of course, perfect) pinched over mere baby talk. "Ooh," her mother would gush, "aren't you a precious angel, and a genius too. Darling, don't you think that our little girl is an absolute gem!" "Naturally," her father echoed, "our princess is one in a million, the best of the best!" Not only parents but various aunts, uncles, and even complicit neighbors heaped sugary praise on the child for the most ordinary of acts, and read great wisdom into them.

A mutual dislike between the two girls stemmed from an argument some years back, when Druzina had called Kedra a potted plant. Kedra in return referred to Druzina as a troglodyte, a put down that Vreena was pleased to share. At the time neither fully understood what the words meant, and no one could recall what sparked the confrontation. But the details hardly mattered; some people, it seems, are forever destined to be at odds.

"And which adventure did she describe?" Lilliwan wondered.

"Adventure?" corrected Kedra. "She simply wrote, in all capital letters, 'WHY SHOULD A PEDE TRAM GO THE WRONG WAY – AREN'T WE BEYOND THAT?' That's *soulless*," she proclaimed.

"Bravo!" echoed Aunt Vreena, who also had taught them this particular denunciation. "Well, you know what they say: opinions are like brackawack berries — some are riper than others."

"And some are downright rotten!" Kedra protested, still taking her rival's triumph as proof that the entire Glen had come unhinged.

"School is *suffocating* me," added Fruku, calling up another of their aunt's signature gripes.

Not knowing what to say further, Vreena then made an assessment of far-reaching significance. "It seems that you have a case of," she began, pausing to lower her voice to a whisper, "Wonkus."

"Wonkus?" cried the twins in unison. "Whatever is that?"

"Well," Vreena explained, winking to Lilliwan, "it's Vonkus, only more so, and similar to Xonkus, but slightly less."

Between Vonkus and Xonkus! The twins weren't sure exactly what that meant, but they didn't like the sound of it at all. Their minds quickly turned to imagining horrible remedies, such as proddings with needles and forced feedings of green leafy vegetables. "How can we, how can we?" Kedra gulped.

"Unwonkus?" guessed Vreena. Fruku, wide-eyed, nodded silently.

"There is only one known cure," answered their aunt, by now an expert in the malady. "And that is getting out of a rut."

"But we're not in a rut!" the twins protested.

"Of course you are," countered Vreena, "otherwise why would you have Wonkus?" Well, then, there simply was no arguing with that type of logic. "Do you have a plan for un-rutting yourselves?"

"Children, why don't you go outside for some fresh air," Lilliwan suggested. After they left she gave her sister an admonishing stare that conveyed, in so many words, *Why must you always stir them up?* Vreena, already becoming attached to the idea of Wonkus, grudgingly promised to put the twins' minds to rest a bit later.

∽⌣

Kedra and Fruku had by then gathered their oddball and set off in the direction of the Enchanted Forest. Why they had chosen that path they could not say, for superstition held that as evening approached mischievous dryads awoke. Perhaps in despair they were not thinking clearly. Possibly they wanted to test their courage. Or maybe they felt an irresistible need to tempt fate. In any case, off they marched.

At last Fruku broke the silence. "What is Wonkus, anyway?"

"It's, um," Kedra paused, "what can *bonk* us."

"And *conk* us and *clonk* us!" added Fruku, evidently pleased with himself. The twins then locked arms, marching in rhythm while chanting, "Oh, Wonkus will bonk us and conk us and clonk us!"

After several repeats of the rhyme they felt their spirits lightened, though not entirely. "Silly Questions?" Fruku proposed.

"Silly Questions!" Kedra enthusiastically agreed. "You go first."

Fruku began in accordance with the unwritten rules, of which there were few. One of the twins would try to place the other in a preposterous dilemma, and turns rotated until someone was left speechless or fell into uncontrollable laughter. "Would you rather grow long, floppy jiparix ears, or a giant brackawack berry nose?"

It was a problematic question indeed, but Kedra kept her composure. "Jiparix ears," she answered, "that way I wouldn't have to hear you whine when I bested you!"

"Clever!" Fruku conceded. "Now you."

Kedra wracked her brains for a suitable reprisal. "How would you rather walk, always looking behind you like a screechiwog, or on slippery, slimy blurpog feet?"

"Looking backwards, definitely," Fruku answered. "That way I could watch you falling behind when we race."

Kedra believed she had laid a perfect trap, and was disappointed when Fruku wriggled out of it. "Oh, snap," she said. "Your turn."

Fruku's face contorted as he searched for an inescapable quandary. "Would you rather smell like The Mudupan, or kiss GubuGar?"

"That's disgusting!" Kedra objected. "Why did you have to ask me that? I won't be able to get either terrible thought out of my mind."

"Because," answered Fruku matter of factly, "I prefer winning to losing."

But the game would have ended then in any case, for they came to the edge of the woods. "Let's play here," Fruku said. On the first throw the oddball bounded over rock and fern, settling inside the grove of knotty jinjibars. The second heave took the twins deeper into the forest. Fruku again tossed the oddball high in the air. It landed with a loud thump, first careening this way, then that. As it finally sprang improbably through a hole in a tree, Kedra could have sworn that she heard a scream. "What was that?" she asked nervously.

"What?"

"A spirit!"

"Don't be silly" Fruku admonished, striding forward. "If you're worried that the tree is haunted, there's no such . . . ." But he didn't have the chance to finish his thought – this time there was no doubt. "WHO DARES TO DISTURB MY TRANQUILITY?" came a menacing cackle.

"Let's go!" Kedra pleaded, taking a nervous step back. Fruku needed little convincing at that point, and the twins raced for the cover of a nearby bush.

Kedra whispered, after catching her breath, "Are we safe here?"

"It might see us if we move," warned Fruku. And so the twins crouched side by side, hoping not to attract further attention.

When several moments passed in silence, Kedra asked, "What do you think that was?"

"I have no idea." Fruku's tone betrayed both fear and the hope of retrieving his toy from whatever cast the ominous voice. At last his curiosity overcame him and he rose slowly until his eyes reached just over the top of the bush.

Though unsure what to expect, he could not have been prepared for the sight that greeted him. "Kedra," he exclaimed, "it's only a mouse!"

"A mouse?" she repeated. "How can that be?"

"Look for yourself." True enough, a rodent had climbed up the interior and stood, proud as day, in the opening. Her bespectacled eyes and tapered nose swept left to right, and then she rubbed her paws together in a self-congratulatory manner before disappearing into the hollows.

"I'm going back," Fruku declared.

Kedra still hesitated. "Are you sure that's wise?"

Fruku was shaken, but resolute. "I'm not about to let a creature that small keep me from the oddball, even if it does talk." Summoning courage he peered into the hole. "Ouch!" he cried, withdrawing abruptly and rubbing his forehead.

"There are plenty more where that came from," threatened the mouse. And then another pebble shot from the hole, glancing off Fruku's cheek.

Fruku smartly stepped to the side. "Look," he offered. "We don't mean any harm."

"You don't mean any harm, you say? You should have thought about that before you sent this horrible egg smashing into my home! That's a fine how do you do if ever I heard one. Now go, or I'll give you a proper pummeling."

"I am truly sorry, and don't intend any disrespect. But do you really think that's such a wise idea, considering . . . ."

"I've dealt with much bigger, you know," the mouse cut him off. "And better you hold your tongue, before you send me into a full-blown rage that you'll not soon forget!"

"I didn't throw the ball there, actually," Fruku protested. "It just bounced that way."

"Well, you ought to be more careful," the mouse scolded Fruku, though with a softened tone.

"I promise." Then, changing tack, he added, "Maybe you could teach me. You seem to have excellent aim."

The mouse suddenly popped out of the hole. "That's true, of course," she exclaimed. "A one-woman tour de force, that's what I am! Though you'd never guess my age. How old do you think I am?"

Fruku, like most boys, wasn't sure how to handle such a question. "Um," he stammered.

"Exactly 327, give or take – I might have misplaced a few years here and there along the way, but no matter. You wouldn't expect an old lady to bean you in the noggin like that, would you? Yet I can toss as well as anyone."

Fruku was speechless. "Well?" chided the mouse, "having made a mess of everything, do you at least plan to introduce yourself? That might go a long way to making amends, you know. Or don't they teach manners these days?"

"I'm Fruku," he obliged. "And this is my twin sister, Kedra."

"Twins, you claim!" came the skeptical reply. "How can that be? She looks like a princess, and you are a common ruffian."

"I like her already" declared Kedra, finally stepping forward. Then, turning to the mouse, she added, "It's very nice to meet you. May I ask your name?"

"Eminalda Spunkyfers Imprudentia Roustabout Bilious Irascibella. Dame Eminalda, to groveling acquaintances."

"How shall we call you?"

"There can hardly be any standing on ceremony with home wreckers. I suppose that Eminalda will have to do. That's what my friends call me. Or at least they would," she qualified, "if there were any."

"You don't have friends?" Kedra asked, though privately she was not entirely surprised.

"Well, not here, anyway. I'm new to this forest."

"Where are you from?" Fruku wondered.

"From there," she answered, gesturing with a tiny arm toward the Tryg Massif.

"That's not *so* far away," contradicted Fruku.

"For you, maybe," Eminalda quipped. "Try marching on *these* legs and say that."

"Point taken," he conceded. "That would be a long walk indeed for a mouse."

Eminalda again took exception. "A *shrew*, if you please – a pocket shrew, to be more precise. Mice are more bashful, not nearly as wily, and what's more, as everyone should know, in comparison with pocket shrews they make at best second-rate herbalists. I come from a long and distinguished line, you know. Though I always wanted to be a stage performer. Would you like to hear my rendition of 'A Bonny Bright Day in the Glen'? It's simply stunning!"

"Another time, perhaps," Kedra demurred. Then, seizing on Eminalda's prior boast, her eyes lit up. "Can you cure diseases, by any chance?"

"Can I cure diseases?" Eminalda repeated, as if her reputation preceded her. "That's like asking if a GubuGar likes mud! There isn't a single one that's a match for Eminalda, if I do say so myself. Why do you ask?"

Fruku wasn't entirely comfortable discussing their condition. "Kedra, I'm not sure we should say anything," he whispered.

"Come now, no one likes a fusspot," Eminalda reproached him. "Don't you suppose that a lady of 328 years, give or take, has not seen just about everything by now?"

"We have Wonkus," Kedra admitted over Fruku's objection.

"Wonkus? No, never heard of it. At least not that I can recall."

"That's a pity," Kedra sighed. "I was hoping that you might have a cure."

"Of course I do," Eminalda boasted. "Or I can make one, anyway. It's just a question of mixing a little bit of this, a modicum of that, and maybe a dollop of the other thing. Eventually I'll find the right formula. Naturally, you might become jaundiced or grow some unsightly hair first, but that's a risk we'll have to take. Let me go root around my cabinets, which, I suppose, might be turned upside down."

"Goodness," said Kedra with alarm. "I hope we haven't damaged your belongings."

"Well, you're lucky. I moved in with only a suitcase, and it seems to have been spared. But just imagine if there *were* furniture – your eggball . . ."

"*Odd*ball" Fruku insisted.

"Your *egg*ball would have smashed it all to bits. I'd have no place to drink tea, would I?"

"Again, I'm very sorry about that. Now if you don't mind, I'll just . . ."

"Oh, do you really need it back?" Eminalda pleaded, her teeny eyes fluttering. "It would make a top-notch punching bag, cushiony and just the right size."

Fruku might have pressed the issue if not for his sister's insistent gaze. "Fine," he conceded. "You're welcome to keep it."

Eminalda clamped her tiny paws together with delight. "Oh, that's simply marvelous of you. I haven't had a present for the longest time! Don't worry," she assured Fruku, "I'll take great care of the eggball – when I'm not pounding the stuffing out of it, anyway. You'll see. Only next time you visit," she entreated, "no flying objects, please. Just call my name – that would be much more civil."

"Agreed," Fruku said.

"Until then" Kedra added.

"Ta-ta, children." *Well*, thought Eminalda, *they are good kids after all, if a bit impulsive. Consequently*, she realized, *we'll get on famously!* And with that fortuitous thought she crawled down for a sparring match with her accidental gift.

CHAPTER 3

Signs of Warning, Signs of Hope

in which the twins engage in sky gazing, their
restraint seems to confirm affliction with Wonkus,
and an old show speaks to them of heroism

"Fruku, wake up." Kedra paused, and after a second try failed to stir her brother, abruptly pulled the sheet off him.

"What, who?" was all Fruku could manage, for it was still early, particularly on a day without school. He opened his eyes momentarily. As the listless furry heap of Jax came into focus he quite agreed that problems should have the decency not to announce themselves this soon. And so he turned over, placing a pillow on his head to block the morning sunlight.

But Kedra was not in a mood to be put off easily. "Fruku," she persisted, "I need to talk to someone."

"Can't you bother Mom or Dad?" her brother protested.

"No," she replied. "Listen, I was thinking about yesterday, and wasn't sure whether we actually met a talking shrew or I was only dreaming. And if Eminalda is real, I can hardly say so to our parents, can I?"

"She's real," Fruku confirmed, painfully noting the empty space on his dresser where his oddball had rested. "And *I'd* like to be dreaming," he quipped. But by now he was sufficiently alert to understand that only he could help, and no less importantly, that Kedra would not leave him in peace until he did. Thus Fruku grudgingly rose and stretched his arms.

"Let's go for a walk," Kedra suggested.

"Now? But Mom and Dad are not up yet. We shouldn't simply disappear."

"We'll leave them a note," Kedra assured him. "And it's not as if the Glen is a dangerous place. Nothing bad ever happens here. Except maybe for screechiwog attacks," she qualified, "and we are already beyond that."

Minutes later the twins were ambling through the gentle hills of their neighborhood, by the quiet, rotund homes that stood in perfect harmony with the landscape. But Kedra's thoughts were on higher matters. "Let's look at the clouds," she proposed. She was fond of spending her time this way, particularly when, as now, she wanted to free her mind. Ideas may be like those billowy mists, Lilliwan had once explained, nondescript at first and coalescing into the most lucid of images.

At last they reached a clearing. Fruku, not yet fully resigned to being out of bed, was more than happy to lie down in the soft grass. Wispy white formations floated above, moving slowly southward. Scanning the heavens, Fruku's gaze fell on a dark blanket hovering at a distance over the northern mountains. "Those are nimbus," he noted. "Pappa says that they bring rain."

"Tomorrow, maybe," replied Kedra, refusing to admit any bad news into their private talk. "Let's better look at the cottony ones above, and try to spot the most interesting shape."

Brian T. Gill

The children found each passing cloud beautiful in its own right, but for some time could not discern anything familiar in the shifting patterns. As they waited, Kedra asked suddenly, "Do you know what I wonder? I've been thinking about the old western walls."

"What about them?"

"Well, to start, why were they built?"

"Maybe farmers didn't want their cattle to wander off," suggested Fruku, holding back a yawn.

"Or maybe they kept invaders away," added Kedra. "Or they might have protected against flooding. The point is, exciting or not, there must be a reason. And walls don't simply fall down either, unless they aren't needed, or are thought to be useless, anyway. In any case, isn't it strange that no one talks about them?"

"Now that you mention, it, yes," Fruku agreed. "There were walls, now there are piles of stones, and that's the end of discussion. If you try to press further, I suppose most will look at you as if you have a third eyeball."

The twins fell into silence until the leading end of an oval, floating somewhere over the brackawack fields, split in two. "That looks like GubuGar," said Fruku proudly. "See? It even has a nose on the right side, and a kind of mouth on the left."

48

"True!" Kedra agreed. "And over there is a screechiwog," she said, pointing to a pudgy form with feathery tufts trailing. "Except that it is flying in the wrong direction."

"Frontward, you mean? Maybe that's the *right* direction," Fruku remarked. "Doesn't it ever seem to you that *forward* and *backward* are not so easy to tell apart?"

Kedra's brow furrowed, a telltale sign that she was deep in reflection. "All the time, I suppose. And up and down, left and right, too. Maybe that's why I feel unsettled lately. Don't you?"

"Well, yes, actually," Fruku admitted. "But I guess that's to be expected, when we have Wonkus."

Kedra might have pressed further had a drifting cloud not recalled their encounter the evening before. "Look," she said, "that one resembles Eminalda." True to her word, an erstwhile formless ball transformed into their new acquaintance, complete with a slender nose and a tiny fist held high.

Fruku had to admit that Kedra spotted the most lifelike figure. "Only," he noted, "she's much smaller in person."

"The cloud is the size of her voice," Kedra laughed. A serious expression then returned to her face. "Fruku, you know we have to keep this to ourselves. No one will ever believe that we actually met a talking pocket shrew."

Fruku nodded reluctantly. It struck him as unfair that he should need to withhold such a fascinating discovery, yet there was no denying that Kedra was right. Resolving not to breathe one word of their experience, the twins rose and began walking home.

Wiggiwump Village had sprung to life in the meantime. Among those Kedra and Fruku passed were young children skipping rope to a popular rhyme. The two on the ends would say:

> *Should you chance upon The Mudupan*
> *Beat a fast retreat*
> *For the first on whom it feasts*
> *Are those not fleet of feet.*

> *It'll sniff you with its eager schnoz,*
> *Clutch you in its hairy paws,*
> *Gnash you into tiny bits,*
> *Or roast you later on a spit!*

In turn, the kids jumping in the middle mocked the naysayers:

> *But we'll never see The Mudupan*
> *Because it's fast asleep.*
> *For a hundred years it rests in a cave*
> *In Tryg Mountain, dark and deep.*

And again, the first two would caution:

> *Still, concerning The Mudupan*
> *It's best to stay far clear.*
> *For it's wretched and mean*

And huge – to wit, four yards from ear to ear.

You best beware its pointy claws
And double so its jagged jaws,
It's razor teeth will slice you through
When still alive or boiled in stew!

Lastly, those skipping would insist:

Should we come across The Mudupan –
But fear not, we never will.
For it slumbers in its hideaway
Huddling, quiet and still.

Under other circumstances Kedra and Fruku might have paid greater attention. But one small flesh-and-bones improbable creature was quite enough for them, and so they continued on, with their thoughts on more immediate matters.

When they arrived home Apseron was fast at work in his laboratory. The kitchen burst with the welcoming aromas of tea, brackawack pancakes, and bacon, which, surprisingly, had not enticed Jax down from his resting place on the upper floor. Lilliwan, expecting the twins to return from their early walk with energetic steps, immediately noticed their quiet demeanors. To be fair, they were neither pouty nor aloof. It was merely that, as they had agreed, there was no credible way to broach a talking shrew! And so they kept a low profile, hoping to avoid attention or any probing into their whereabouts the prior evening.

When their silence continued at breakfast, Lilliwan begun to worry that they could, in fact, have Wonkus (or at least the essence of it, if under a different name). In reply to questions on their wellbeing she received terse answers such as "fine," which might carry any number of meanings, including quite the opposite. The short shrift only further aroused her suspicion that not all was in order.

Their spirits lifted only when Apseron's mother called unexpectedly. "Nana!" they exclaimed, rushing to give her a big hug. "How are the world's greatest Grandkids?" she asked, wrapping her arms around them.

"Good," Kedra replied, upon which Lilliwan's eyebrow raised yet again. She wanted to say considerably more, of course, but held herself back. Fruku simply nodded.

"Listen, children," Lilliwan interjected. "Why don't you run off for a minute."

"But Nana only just arrived," Fruku protested.

"Don't worry," their Grandma assured them. "I can stay for some time. Here," she added, reaching into her bag, "take these with you." She handed each a homemade brackawack muffin. The bushes in her garden had yielded the first ripe berries, which she picked fresh earlier that morning.

"What will we do?" asked Kedra, also not wanting to leave the kitchen.

Fruku glanced at his watch. "It's time for 'Captain Luminous!'" he declared. The serial, in black-and-white, dated from the time before Wiggiwumps were expected to reason with treachery, and were allowed to administer a good boxing on the nose when justice so demanded. Thus had the program been swept away by the changing tide of history and mores. Fruku was among the dwindling number who still watched, and proudly at that.

The twins settled onto the couch. When the lead-in started Fruku mouthed the words by heart: *"Fear not when darkness descends, for no shadow, however sinister, can abide the surpassing brilliance of . . ."* Then he paused before delivering the clincher, *"Captain Luminous!"* On cue the hero appeared, proudly thrusting forward his chest before catching his leaping assistant, Highgloss.

"That's too much," Kedra jibed. "A jumping *Jiparix*! Really, who would believe that?"

"Silence, miscreant" Fruku proclaimed, "or you shall be punished for your insolence!"

"Ooh, I'm frightened," Kedra mocked. "What will you do, throw your muffin at me? Seriously, who talks like that anyway?"

"Really, Kedra, please – it's starting" Fruku implored, "and I haven't seen this one."

At the same time the elders began a discussion that had both nothing and everything to do with the episode under way. "Are the kids alright?" asked Grandma, sensing concern on the part of their Mother.

"I'm not sure," Lilliwan replied. "They've been acting strangely lately."

"Have they done something wrong?"

"Oh no, it's not like that," Lilliwan assured her. "It's just that . . . how can I explain?"

Grandma sensed that she might know how to finish the thought. "You don't feel that they are thriving," she offered.

"Yes," Lilliwan confirmed, "that's it. They seem to be stuck somehow. And I don't understand, because they truly are exceptional children."

"Maybe they're stuck *because* they are exceptional." Lilliwan considered the proposition, finding that she could neither accept nor dismiss it outright. "It would seem that the brightest children most easily find their places in the sun," Grandma continued, "but that's seldom the case. Take Apseron, for example." Lilliwan nodded, recalling how as a schoolboy he suffered for his aptitude. She could still remember the laughter when he first proposed to build a moving irrigation system, which years later took shape as a village centerpiece. "No doubt he would have been accepted earlier if he were more conventional. But he insisted on doing things his own way. In the end he gained appreciation. Don't worry about the kids. Sooner or later they will find their strides too."

Lilliwan smiled. The conversation lifted the heaviness, although she couldn't entirely shake the sensation that difficulties lay ahead.

"As we left off," returned the deep voice of the narrator, *"our hero was preparing to enter the abandoned lurdite shaft, convinced that the Constable's daughter waited there to reveal the identity of the masked bank robber."*

"Cordella?" the hero whispered.

The front door slammed shut with a loud metallic thud. *"You need not worry about her,"* came a jarring reply from the dim recesses. *"She is safe – unlike you!"*

"Naughty Speckle, I might have known!"

"It's too late for that now," taunted the arch villain. *"As I expected, you couldn't resist an invitation from pure, pretty Cordella."*

"Ew," Fruku interjected. "Why do they need to ruin the show with mushy stuff?"

"It's the only part I like," responded Kedra, although the question was not addressed to anyone in particular.

"After all, your nobility is also your greatest weakness," the *Naughty Speckle continued. "But enough sentimentality - let us now see the trap into which you have leapt!"* There was the sound of a lever, and then the room lit up, revealing a diminutive

captor holding an odd, oversized pistol. *"In case you are wondering, the puddle you're standing in is quick-setting rubber."*

"Up to my knees," acknowledged Captain Luminous, *"or head level to you."*

"Quiet!" the villain snapped. *"Although it hardly matters. Soon the great protector of the Glen will be no more. Have you any last words to say for yourself?"*

"Yes," answered the Captain nonchalantly, *"you're jealous because I eclipse you."*

Initially taken aback, *"Well, yes, in fact I am,"* the Naughty Speckle confessed. *"There's nothing for you to gain hearing this all now, so let me tell you: I envy your self-confident smugness, to the point of being driven mad by it. I covet your popularity and adoration. And while we're at it, I even resent how your cape flaps so dashingly in the wind, without wrinkling. It's unfair that you were blessed with all the roguish looks and charm! But I have an equalizer, and that is a devious mind and a lack of scruples."*

"That would be *two* equalizers," Kedra noted.

"Sh!" Fruku admonished.

"Finally," reveled the Naughty Speckle, *"I will bring you down to my level. Meet the instrument of your doom, the Infantizer!"* *"Would you like to know what it does?"* he asked after a round of maniacal laughter subsided.

"No, to be honest. I'm not interested."

"Not even a little?" The villain seemed both surprised and hurt.

"No," the Captain reaffirmed, *"not at all."*

"Well, I'm going to tell you anyway!" the Naughty Speckle shouted. *"When I said that 'I will bring you down to my level,' I meant, quite literally, that I will bring you down to my level. I might not possess your good qualities, Captain, but I can have the next best thing, which is to deprive you of them. You see, the Infantizer ages everything in reverse. After a sustained blast you will become a pale comparison of your former self, a little baby, crawling and spitting up."*

"You won't get away with this, Naughty Speckle!"

"Oh, but I already have," insisted the villain, who began to take aim.

"Sorry to spoil your plans, but when I said earlier that 'I might have known,' I meant, literally, that I might have known. And you've let me stall just long enough." At that Highgloss, sent ahead through the back entrance, pounced on the Naughty Speckle from beyond. The Infantizer flew through the air, landing, conveniently, in the outstretched arm of Captain Luminous. *"Great job, boy,"* he said, *"keep this scoundrel busy while I free myself."* He then pointed the ray at the rubber, which, aging backward, returned to liquid, and stepped triumphantly from the puddle just as Highgloss released the undersized villain from his jaws. *"I'll take this from here,"* he said, grabbing the Naughty Speckle. *"Go tell the Constable that a bundle of joy is waiting for him."* He then hung his vanquished

foe on a nail, by his shorts. *"You'll have plenty of time to contemplate the error of your ways from the confines of a prison cell."*

"Curse you, Captain Luminous!" shouted the Naughty Speckle, defiantly shaking his fist as the curtain closed. *"You've beaten me at my own game, and at wordsmithing to boot."*

"So children," returned the voice of the narrator, with Fruku joining in, *"we have come to the end of our story. Another adventure awaits. Until then, remember to keep to the light."*

"And" interjected Captain Luminous, *"our moral for this week is: don't be afraid to take initiative."*

"Right as rain!" exclaimed Fruku.

Kedra's response was more cautious. "I don't know," she added. "No good deed goes unpunished."

"Who says that?"

"Who *doesn't?*" Kedra asked. "Hardly anyone wants to take action. Do you realize why you watch 'Captain Luminous'"?

"Because it's the greatest show ever!"

"No," Kedra replied, "Because nothing like it has been made since Mom and Dad were kids. The heroes have all disappeared."

The thought weighed heavily on Fruku. "That's true, isn't it?" he replied with a hint of sadness. Yet as we shall see, the message stayed with him.

C

The twins bounded back into the kitchen, just as Lilliwan and Nana had finished their talk. "How was the show?" Grandma asked.

"Excellent," Fruku replied, continuing the single-word pattern. Lilliwan noted that the new state of being was nonetheless an upgrade from "fine." For her part, Kedra was less impressed, but sparkled from the enjoyment of needling her brother.

"I'll have to go now, kids," Grandma added. "Gardening calls."

"But Nana," Fruku protested, "we barely saw you!"

"Can we stay with you for the night?" Kedra asked, making her best jiparix eyes.

"Well," answered their Grandma, "it's fine with me if your Mother agrees." Now, as children instinctively know, the alliance between grandparents and grandkids is prescribed by nature itself. Should the middle generation find itself in opposition, it will almost certainly be outflanked by one side or the other. So when, with Nana's approval the twins trained their pleading stares on Lilliwan, there was no practical way for her to refuse.

"You may," she agreed, secretly pleased with their resourcefulness. "I have a rehearsal later. Dad will take you early evening."

"Hurrah!" the twins yelled. They said hasty goodbyes before running off to pack their things.

CHAPTER 4

Deeper Connections with the Past

in which a visit to the Grandparents provides welcome distractions, including reminiscences and a still hoarier tale

The time could hardly pass quickly enough for the twins, and as 12-year olds are disposed to do they repeatedly glanced at the clock. *It's unfair,* thought each more than once, *that in school a minute often seems like an hour, and while waiting for fun, an hour seems like a day.* For her part, Nana had worked ceaselessly to put the house in order, and barely finished before they arrived.

As they walked up the path, Apseron started to say, "Now kids," intending to remind them to be perfect guests. But Kedra and Fruku sprinted away the moment Nana and Grandpa opened the door.

"What would you like to do?" Grandpa asked after greeting them. He soon realized the risk in such an open-ended invitation, for the twins had dreamed up an entire list.

"We'd like to have tea, as always" Fruku began. A puckish glint then showed in his eye. "And to hear about Dad when he was little." At that Apseron suppressed a grimace, which prompted a conspiratorial smile from his own parents. "Oh, and about the first settlers of the Glen."

"And," continued Kedra, "to tell fortunes, to stay up late, of course, and to hear a story."

"That's a very ambitious agenda," Nana responded with amusement. "We'd better go soon if we want to manage even half of it." The twins then quickly said farewell to Apseron and bounded inside.

"Grandma?" Fruku inquired, wasting no time at all.

"Yes, Fruku."

"Is it true that Poppa and Mayor Tuggles were classmates?"

"Yes, all through school."

"Who was smarter?" Fruku prompted, smiling impishly.

"Your Father, of course," Grandma answered. "To be honest, Gapron was never much of a student. He always asked your Dad for help with his homework."

"Why isn't Poppa the mayor, then?" wondered Kedra.

"Well, your Father always believed that . . . how can I put it?"

Grandpa laughed, recalling Apseron's youthful pronouncement. "'Engineering is no place for dull minds,' he liked to declare, 'so leave room for them in city hall.'"

Kedra twitched her nose, her telltale sign of perplexion. "But why should such a man be the mayor?"

"Because," Grandma explained. "Your Father once said a politician is harmless, like a conductor."

"You mean like Momma," Kedra added.

"That was before he met her, of course," Grandma clarified. "And it's well that he did – scientists with no sense for art have worked more than enough mischief on the Glen."

"As he explained it then," Grandpa continued, "the conductor is a man with wild hair and an irrelevant stick. The musicians know how to ignore his crazy gestures and stay on the beat – why, they probably would play just fine if the conductor left. Nonetheless, they are happy to let him take the bow, as long as the performance held together. In the end, that's all that counts."

And so the conversation wrapped up with each convinced that Gapron Tuggles hadn't room in his head for a single idea, useful or otherwise. Little could they have known that the mayor, at that very moment, was occupied with interior design. Normally, of course, home decoration would not be a cause for alarm, though in this case it was bound to set in motion a consequential sequence of events. But we will need to leave the odd particulars to later chapters, for it was becoming late, and the twins' attention would turn to other matters.

"Read us a bedtime story, Grandpa," Kedra implored.

"A *scary* tale," Fruku requested.

"A *fairy tale*," challenged Kedra.

"Let me see," said Grandpa, stroking his chin. "Maybe I can find one that both of you will like." He then set out to his treasured library, while Grandma sent the twins to change for the night.

There is, to be a sure, a basic format to a bedtime story: the reader reads, the listeners listen, and the line between them is nicely demarcated. But it was not so with the twins. Their eager, curious minds absorbed every detail and wished to know the reason behind each. Such were the questions they posed that adults, who had left knowledge of most truly important matters behind in their youth, could provide no ready answers. And so as Grandpa perused the shelves he searched for other materials that might come in handy.

In a moment he returned with a stack of books. The spine of the faded tome atop the pile made a cracking sound when opened, sending a thin layer of dust flying. "Yes, I think this will do nicely." Grandpa furrowed his brow. "But I do have to warn you, it's truly frightening. Are you sure you'll be able to sleep?"

Kedra was not certain, but decided to keep quiet. "Of course!" Fruku replied confidently.

"That's what your Dad thought, too. Well, then." *Deep in the belly of a craggy karst*, Grandpa began.

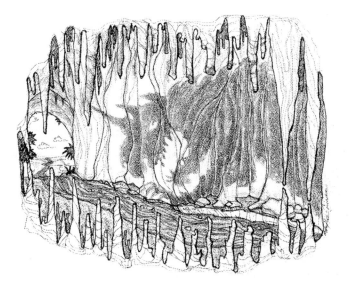

"A what?" Kedra asked.

"Karst," Grandpa repeated, already needing to refer to the dictionary brought for comfort. "A jagged network of tunnels carved out by water." He continued: *in the foreboding dank hollows, there dwelt an abomination . . .*

Now it was Fruku's turn. "What's that?" he inquired.

"A creature so hideous that its very existence was an offense to all that is good and decent," Grandpa explained, this time extemporizing. "You see," he added, breaking character, "there was a time when people knew such words. That was when schools still taught fundamentals, and left self-esteem to parents. But I digress. Where was I? Oh yes . . ." *The clip-clop of its cloven hooves would echo ominously throughout the forsaken caverns, which the beast paced in spiteful agitation.*

"And how did he look?" asked Kedra, betraying a combination of nervousness and fascination that resides most comfortably in children.

"Patience," Grandpa counseled. *For it both craved and resented the upper world, the serene beauty of which stood in aching contrast to its own incurable hideousness.* "Mm, we're coming to your question, I think – though you might well wish that we didn't." *And woe to whomsoever gazed upon the creature, for wretched it was indeed! The beady, crimson eyes of the beast seemed to burn with the intensity of hell itself. Sulfur fumes spewed through flared nostrils at the fore of its ever-probing nose.*

It is said the only beings that could bear this surpassing gruesomeness were the blind newts slithering along the soggy floors. But their sightlessness was of fleeting worth, for the unfortunate laggards that failed to scatter upon the fulsome approach were grabbed and thrown, mercilessly, into the beast's gaping maw. "Myum myum myum," Grandpa smacked his lips while the twins squealed "Uggh!" in revulsion.

"Well, children, this isn't too much for you, is it?" Grandpa paused. "I can stop if you wish." The twins silently shook their heads. "No? Bravo!" *From the shoulders draped a necklace of skeletons, threaded together through holes that the creature poked with its spiky claws. So great was the number of hapless victims that the bones hung nearly down to its backwards-bending knees.*

Yet for many years the abomination was confined to its cursed lair. Only in the countryside, where folk kept their ancestors in their hearts, did the tales still bear credence. In the hamlet, one generation, enduring the terror of its stalking, passed on the lore, sparing no detail. The next in line faithfully conveyed the message to their children, although not from a personal account. In turn the third generation knew not whether to heed the warnings, and the fourth doubted the stories altogether. Thus with time the masses felt shielded by the thin veneer of their goodwill, and most who yet called for vigilance were denounced as fools.

This sentiment was shared not least of all by King Baldafor the Younger, an affable but unwise ruler whose dominion extended over the hamlet and karst. As fate had it, the King was soon to celebrate the marriage of his daughter, Altanoria.

"Finally," Kedra exclaimed, "something interesting." Fruku simply rolled his eyes and hoped that the story would return to the more essential threads.

She was to be wed to a prince from a land with which the King had long sought an alliance. Altanoria's beauty knew no equal – for it was forbidden that any lass surpass the princess in loveliness. A girl whose eyes gleamed more brightly would be told to avert her gaze, and should her hair be of a greater sheen she was compelled to keep it wrapped. And for her part, if Altanoria was unsatisfied with her reflection, the King would order the offending mirror smashed.

As was the custom, continued Grandpa, *the King summoned all of his subjects to inquire whether any sign might portend badly. On that very day an orphaned farmer boy, a lad of . . ."* Grandpa paused, turning the page.

"Unrivalled handsomeness," Fruku filled in, imagining himself to be the protagonist.

"Of quite *average* looks, and intellect too – nothing to brag about," Grandpa continued, suppressing a smile.

Kedra giggled with enjoyment. "You certainly are fun to provoke," Grandpa chided Fruku. "Continuing on": *common upbringing but extraordinary valor was tending his dray mules, together with his sister . . . ."*

"Certainly *she* was attractive," Kedra interjected.

"I bet she was a fish-faced hag!" Fruku retorted.

"Now, children," admonished Grandpa. "The story isn't about the two of you, actually. Or do you think otherwise? Anyway, let's back up a bit": *together with his sister, whose plain clothing could not diminish her fair charm.* Kedra, predictably, blinked contentedly. *The two cared little of royal matters and gave no thought to an audience with the King.*

But it was not their destiny to remain behind. The first mark of troubles was perceptible only to the dray mules, which commenced nervous braying. When the trembling grew in intensity, they begin to pull madly at their reins. The children, recalling the tales of their forebears, knew how to read the warnings: the creature was again to bring turmoil to the upper world. And so, with trepidation they joined the ranks of the countless supplicants arriving on foot and horse.

"Hear ye, hear ye," initiated the court crier, pounding a staff on the aged cobblestones. "By the bidding of the Good and Just King Baldafor, any soul with cause to believe the blessed ceremony to be inopportune shall step forward."

None of the elders wished to be the bearer of grave news, and thus the silence was broken by a solitary voice from the back of the crowd. "With your indulgence," begged the lad, "I must tell the King of coming unrest."

"Who wishes to speak?" demanded the crier, not yet discerning the source. "Present yourself and state your case."

"I came, Sire," said the boy, making his way to the front, "to warn that the beast stirs." Upon the utterance of these words an uncomfortable hush fell over the court, and the lad felt the concentration of a thousand unappreciative eyes upon him.

"And how come you to believe this possible?" the King, surprised that a mere farm boy should heed the call, at last inquired.

"Because we felt it, Your Majesty," added his sister timidly. "The ground shook beneath our feet." The lull in the audience then gave way to agitated whispers.

The King, disposed to seek counsel from those with only bookish knowledge of the realm, turned to Squire Dobbins, a man of negotiable principles who had thereby curried favor. "What say you to this odd claim?" he asked, lowering his voice.

"We must allay these fears at once, Sire," advised the solicitous squire, "or the union could be jeopardized. And dare I say, moreover, that your guardianship might be called into question."

The malevolent stress placed on the last of these words had the intended effect. "How then shall I put an end to this agitation?" the King entreated.

"We must expose a flaw in their claim," replied the cunning squire, "which judging from their lowly station shall not be difficult. Ask them how, precisely, the earth moved."

"Pray tell," bellowed the King, "what is the nature of this trembling you assert?"

The girl, living closer to the land than did the court, supposed that her reply would be given due consideration. "It shook, Sire, as if under a pounding of hammers," she answered resolutely.

The squire again whispered furtively into the ear of his King. "A pounding of hammers!" Baldafor mocked. "Why, this is nothing more than the settling of soil!" On these words the spectators broke into scornful laughter. And then the King, though not a man of malicious spirit, committed an act of regrettable cruelty that befalls men infirm of spine. "The wedding shall go forward as planned," he proclaimed, "and for this unjustified breach of the peace, the provocateurs are henceforth banished!"

And so the brother and sister turned and left, feeling upon their backs, as they walked away, the resentful gaze of a thousand eyes. The certain knowledge of the misfortune they had failed to avert weighed heavily. "What shall we do now?" the girl asked. "What we can," replied the boy with sorrowful resignation. "We will at least secure our flock from the beast."

By the next day the court had forgotten the dire warnings and turned to preparations for the wedding. The King, sparing no expense, ordered every rose in the land gathered, with the petals spread on processional walkways. From every square the carefree sounds of minstrels echoed. Fish, foul, and game were roasted over no less than a hundred fires.

And then the wind shifted unfavorably, carrying the comingling of aromas in the direction of the beast. Driven mad with yearning, the creature made way to the karst opening. Nearby, its stomping, now more violent, sent the dray mules into a frenzy. "We must do something," pled the girl. "What can we do?" her brother despaired. "If we arrive on time we will be ridiculed. And if we are too late the attempt will be in vain." Yet his sister persisted. "We must try," she declared. Her brother was at first unmoved, and relented only when the girl undertook to ride by herself.

And so the two mounted their fastest horse and rode with the fury of an army, reaching the court just as the wedding was to commence. Their presence occasioned the response the boy had feared. "What outrage is this?" demanded the squire.

"Sire," replied the boy, addressing instead the King, "the creature attacks."

"Have I not cast you out for your insolence?" demanded the King. "For this intrusion upon a sacred event I should have you boiled in oil!"

But the King's rage soon gave way to trepidation, for the stones shook as a long shadow fell over the crowd. "It's the beast!" yelled a voice. A panic ensued. Those who could run took flight or sought cover wherever they could find it, a few, such as Squire Dobbins, passed out from fright, while others stood in place, paralyzed with dread. Among them were King Baldafor and Princess Altanoria, who would have fled but for her dress being cinched too tightly around her robust figure.

The abomination then stepped into the courtyard, searching for its first victims. "Feed on them!" pleaded the King, pointing at the peasant brother and sister, who had bravely held their ground. The merciless gaze of the creature turned their way, and after a moment's hesitation a clawed hand reached for . . .

"The King," implored Fruku as Grandpa turned the page.

"I hope he eats the princess," Kedra added. "She deserves it."

"Well, you're out of luck then," Grandpa chided them. "I'm afraid that he will devour the kids instead. Let's see," he continued, pretending to glance at the book. "Yes, realizing that they would be much more flavorful, the creature swallowed them whole. The end."

"It can't be!" Kedra protested.

"Why not? Must this be a happy tale? If you don't like it, you'll need to write your own." The grin on Grandpa's face again gave him away. "Alright, then": *the trembling King and his daughter, whom, the beast surmised, would taste more like the cave-dwelling crawlers it fancied. The royals screamed ignobly before the abomination dispatched them both with one brusque gulp.*

But it must have found the sensation displeasing, for its belly rumbled violently and it let out a most vile belch. At that Fruku laughed while Kedra made a face of revulsion. *And along with the noxious fumes the beast expelled two shiny objects, a crown and a tiara, that arced into the hands of the boy and girl. The abomination, now sated, cast a final stare about the courtyard, pausing only to collect the limp body of Squire Dobbins. Though of base intellect, the beast rightly sensed him to be pliable, and thus useful as a plaything or perhaps a cleaner of the excretions that wet its cave. Then it stomped back to those lonesome hollows, not to be heard again for many years.*

One by one the relieved guests emerged from hiding to greet their new rulers, who humbly accepted the task of restoring order to the kingdom.

Uttering the words "the end," this time in earnest, Grandpa closed the book. "Now, how did you like the story?" The twins had to admit that they did, very much. Then they lowered their heads onto the pillows as Grandpa tucked them in for the night.

Fruku suddenly remembered the children skipping rope the day before. "Um, Grandpa, The Mudupan is not real, right?" Fruku wanted to know.

"Probably not," Grandpa answered. "When I was a boy, a few older folk claimed to have seen him. But that might have been just to scare young children. If I didn't listen to my Mother, she would tell me to show respect, because otherwise The Mudupan would come for me. Of course nowadays Wiggiwumps don't think like that. Anyway, good night, children. Sweet dreams!" Grandpa patted them on the head a final time and turned out the light.

"Are the children asleep?" asked Grandma when he returned to the kitchen.

"I'm not sure," replied their weary eyed Grandpa, "but the story certainly left *me* exhausted."

"I'll check on them," Grandma offered. As she opened the door she heard them reflecting, in whispers, on the moral of the story.

"Grandma, why are there such things as monsters?" Fruku asked.

"I suppose because if there weren't, we would have no heroes either," she replied. "Wouldn't the world be a dull place then?"

Kedra found the explanation satisfying, but not entirely so. "Does that mean we need to live with monsters?"

"Well no, hopefully not," answered Grandma. "But we do need to stay on our guard. Otherwise, there might be monsters without heroes — and that is the worst of all outcomes."

"And why are there pests in the world," Kedra wondered. She thought of no one in particular but might have named Druzina, Rispard, whom we shall meet presently, and of course GubuGar.

"That's also tricky," admitted Grandma. "Maybe to keep us on alert against the monsters." The twins also thought this explanation to be puzzling. "But that will all have to wait for another day," Grandma added, hoping to coax the last worries out of them with gentle rubs.

"And, Grandma," asked Fruku as sleep closed in, "what does it mean to be a hero?"

Grandma found the depth of the questions astounding. "I suppose," she reflected, "nothing more than stepping forward when no one else will. Goodnight, children."

"Goodnight," they repeated with weary voices.

"Um, Fruku?" Kedra asked after Grandma left the room.

"Yes?"

"Would you mind if we slept with the lamp lit?"

"No," Fruku answered. "I mean, I'd rather not, of course, but if you need it on, that wouldn't bother me too much." Mercifully, within moments they each were dreaming of their own fantastic capers.

CHAPTER 5

The Thin Line between Success and Failure

in which the twins are accused of delusions,
the mayor has a "Grand Idea,"
and a noble gesture goes visibly awry

As the school week started, the fading brackawack petals began to drop. Back in her garden, Grandma walked the rows in search of the most fragrant, to be dried for storing. During the chilly winter months she would boil them on the stove, releasing an aromatic steam that chased away the chilly greyness.

But cold and darkness were yet far off. On this day the Wiggiwumps eagerly awaited the coming yield, soon to be ripe for picking by the bushel. And, as it had since they could remember, this happy occasion meant the approach of Harvest Fest, the largest celebration of this year. In the village center workers were busy unloading tent poles, unfurling fabric, and assembling kiosks and stages. On the fringes, performers practiced with their juggling pins or squeezed into medieval costumes. Presently, cheerful crowds would fill the square, mingling, feasting on their beloved berries, and listening to the musical wonder of Lilliwan, who, despite her earlier reservations, had nearly brought the Glen brass band into perfect form.

Everyone looked forward to the gala – everyone, that is, except for Gapron Tuggles. Shielded from the hustle and bustle outside he nervously watched the belfry clock from his vantage point in Spiral Tower. The hands were circling far too rapidly for his comfort; with only days to go, the final preparations were woefully behind schedule. The mayor had thus spent the early morning pacing frantically, clutching at his tie, twirling a pencil, and, most of all, ruing his decision to name GubuGar the guests of honor. *Jacks of Many Trades?* he thought. *Event Planners? Stuff and nonsense! Why, with two heads between them,* he lamented, *they can't manage to come up with one solitary proposal for putting the gala over the top.* It would only be later that night when Gapron, delayed by inclement weather, had his own flash of inspiration. But we shall come to that fateful moment in due course.

In the Sygard household Lilliwan, glancing out the window, noticed the approaching storm clouds. "It looks like rain," she cautioned the twins as they were readying for school. Her words soon proved well founded, for within minutes the first drops started to fall. Had Fruku and Kedra not walked with open umbrellas over their shoulders they might have heard the footsteps of two classmates, Humberbred and Rispard, following closely behind. Certainly, they then would not have talked openly about a certain pocket shrew.

"Kedra, I've been thinking," Fruku led in to a proposal. "It's really a pity that Eminalda doesn't have a proper home."

"Yes," she agreed, not yet grasping what this thought implied.

"So," continued Fruku, "considering that you aren't using your dollhouse anymore . . . ."

"But I *am*," Kedra interjected. "At least, I might want to," she clarified, hoping not to seem overly attached to her favorite toy.

Humberbred had meant to greet the twins. But his cohort, the class troublemaker, took joy in the thought of a 12-year old girl playing with dolls and wished to hear more. In truth Rispard was less spiteful than bored, though to those he pranked out of tedium the difference mattered little. And the unsuspecting twins would soon provide him with an abundance of joke material.

"I don't mean to give *everything* away," explained Fruku. "But can't you at least spare some furniture?" Recalling Eminalda's various hints and complaints, he imagined that their new companion might indeed be better tempered were her tree hole to be comfortably equipped.

Kedra experienced the particular twinge that comes from knowing what is right, yet feeling an emotional resistance. "But the set is a perfect match for the house," she protested.

"And just the right size for a shrew, too," Fruku noted. At that point the ears of Humberbred and Rispard perked up. Until this moment they had understood Eminalda to be a Wiggiwump – such fuss over a pet would make far more interesting gossip for the playground.

Their curiosity turned to bewildered delight when the twins discussed what the recipient might say in return! "Aspekinshru?" Humberbred muttered, barely stifling a loud snort. "Sh!" warned Rispard, who beamed as if he had unearthed a pot of gold.

"Look," Fruku continued, "I was attached to my oddball. But we shouldn't only think about ourselves. Besides, as Mom and Dad say, sometimes kindness comes back to us."

Kedra finally relented. "Fine," she said, making a slightly pouty face. After a pause she added, still aiming to receive something in return, "Eminalda did mention curing our Wonkus. Do you suppose she has the pills ready by now?"

The conversation dissolved as they approached the school. "Maybe," Fruku answered. "Let's visit her tomorrow." He thought about adding *with a few presents*, but decided against belaboring the point. No sooner had they shaken the water off of their umbrellas when two smug classmates entered behind them. Humberbred mumbled something or other – it was seldom possible to say exactly what, but he seemed unusually upbeat for the foul weather. The twins became further unsettled when they noticed Rispard's devilish grin.

~)(~

Normally at 10:30 Mr. Mramsee would have let the class out for recess. But today the playground, being muddy and full of puddles, was fit only for a GubuGar. And so the students stayed inside, looking with frustration at the downpour. Alas, courtesy of Humberbred and Rispard, they found a release for their pent-up energy.

The first signs of trouble came as whispers. Soon the snickering started. The twins then felt as if their classmates were staring at them. Their fears were confirmed when whomever happened to suppress laughter at that moment broke off eye contact.

Just when their moods hit the bottom (or so they thought), Druzina sauntered over to them, grinning wryly. "Kedra and Fruku," she began, "we all know that you're unpopular. But you don't have to stoop to inventing friends, least of all," she paused for effect, "talking mice!" At that, the whole class fell to sniggering.

"It's a pity that *you're* not imaginary," countered Fruku with noticeable irritation. Though not carefully measured, the words had their intended effect. Druzina winced as some of the jeering turned on her.

The jostling might have continued in the twins' favor had Kedra not emphatically declared, "Eminalda is a *shrew*, and it's none of your business what we discuss with her!"

Druzina sensed that she had caught the twins in an inescapable trap, and the thought pleased her immensely. "So you confess that she talks!" The entire room erupted into full-blown laughter. Only Rispard's boisterous "bwaah hah hah" could be heard over the din.

"Speaking of imaginary creatures," interjected Fruku when the hooting and hawing at last died down, "what's the difference between Rispard and The Mudupan?" His question managed to catch the attention of their tormentors. "One is a large, dimwitted, smelly beast," he continued, "and the other lives in Tryg Mountain!" An uncomfortable hush then fell over the room.

Mercifully, the time allotted for recess had passed. The students filed back to the classroom, led by Rispard, who was smoldering with rage. Druzina, who somehow had heard the earlier retort aimed at her, squinted as if to say, *This isn't over yet!* Only Humberbred lingered behind. "You're jealous because I eclipse you!" said Fruku, quoting Captain Luminous.

"Sootyurself, azyapliz" (or something to that effect) muttered Humberbred, who strutted away unfazed. It wasn't fair, thought Fruku, that a Wiggiwump could escape a good put down like that, merely by not being smart enough to understand it.

The rest of the day could hardly pass quickly enough, and the twins were utterly dejected as they returned from school. It should come as no surprise that GubuGar, with their habit to be in the middle of everything, crossed their path at that very moment. "Hello, kids," Gubu greeted them. "Salutations," added Gar, who, having sniffed the air, deduced the addressees.

"You look a bit downtrodden, if you don't mind me saying so," Gubu suggested.

"That's because we have Wonkus," Kedra replied, instantly regretting her confession.

Fruku, already thin of patience, hoped to bring the conversation to a rapid conclusion. "But I suppose you wouldn't be able to help."

"Of course we would!" proclaimed Gubu, slightly offended. "We are the Factotum of the Glen, after all."

"He means," Gar explained, "that among many other vocations, we are healers of the highest order."

"Well, I am, anyway," Gubu boomed. "You're a quack," he snipped at Gar, who turned up his nose in protest. "Let me have a closer look at you," Gubu continued, focusing his lone eyeball left and right on the twins. "What did you say ails you?"

Kedra thought about retracting her admission, but resigned herself to continuing. "Wonkus," she repeated. "It must be something awful, because no one wants to tell us about it."

"Oh, it's quite serious, to be certain," agreed Gubu confidently.

"Then you've heard of Wonkus?" Kedra demanded.

"Oh no, never," replied Gubu. "But it sounds miserable indeed!"

Fruku's wish to be spared further inanity might then have been granted if Gar did not again contradict the Gubu head. "For *my* part, I am well versed in this particular malady. Tell me, what, exactly are your symptoms?"

"Dizziness, and not thinking very clearly," Fruku replied, looking at his sister.

"And irritability," she shot back, returning the disapproving stare.

"A tendency to drag others into problems," jabbed Fruku.

"And a complete lack of support and sympathy," returned Kedra.

"Exactly as I expected!" declared Gubu, forgetting that he had renounced all knowledge of Wonkus. "The only question is which strain applies, minor or major."

"*Mildus* or *extremus*," Gar added authoritatively. "Those are the proper medical terms."

"So which is it?" Kedra asked.

"Well, definitely the more severe variety, I'm afraid," Gubu concluded.

Gar dissented. "I don't agree with your diagnosis. Let's put this to a vote!"

"Fine," Gubu conceded. "All in favor of the extreme case, say aye. Aye! And all opposed, say nay."

"Nay!" Gar shouted.

"Blast," bemoaned Gubu, "another tie!"

"We'll have to flip for it, then," Gar offered.

"You haven't a Brack to your name," Gubu remarked snidely, "let alone a pocket to keep it in."

"That's cruel of you!" objected Gar. "Though, as for not owning clothes befitting my station in life, I shall take your proposition into account."

"So what exactly is your conclusion?" Fruku asked, visibly annoyed.

"Let us sum up," replied Gar. "Either you do or you do not have a serious condition."

"Which may or may not be curable," added Gubu. "But in any case," he offered, "try not to be too bothered. Just get plenty of rest," he pronounced. "And tea. Oh, and stay away from sharp objects."

"Avoid ladders," Gar volunteered. "Slippery surfaces, too. That's the main thing, where either strain is concerned!"

Fruku was about to challenge the so-called healers. But, preempting any further questioning, GubuGar congratulated themselves on their illuminating performance and slithered away. The twins suspected the banter to be codswallop, yet being unable to prove it as such were left with anxiety. In their defense, even more preposterous ideas may take hold in Throgwottum Glen, as we shall see.

The twins arrived soaked through and wearing matching downcast expressions. "How was your day?" Lilliwan inquired when they entered.

Kedra tried admirably to seem sincere. "Fine," she replied politely.

"We'd rather not talk about it, actually," said Fruku. Kedra, not wanting openly to emulate the quarreling two-headed meddler they had just met on the road, settled for giving her brother another disapproving look.

"Heavens," declared Lilliwan. "Whatever happened?"

"Everything that possibly could go wrong, did," Fruku bemoaned.

Lilliwan took their wet jackets. "Why don't you dry off first and then tell me." Minutes later, dressed more comfortably but still looking disheveled, the twins descended the stairs. "Now," continued their mother, "what exactly put you in such a state?"

"Everyone laughed at us today." Kedra's voice conveyed both anger and hurt.

"Everyone?"

"Everyone!" cried the twins in unison.

"Especially Humberbred," Kedra added, "and Rispard, and that terrible, horrible, no-good Druzina!" Kedra found it grossly unjust that such a person should exist, or at least that she should have to suffer her company.

"Why?" Lilliwan wanted to know.

"Because," Fruku volunteered, "they find it funny that we have . . ." He nearly let slip *a talking shrew as a friend*, but caught himself in the nick of time. "Well," he stammered, "different, um, ways of understanding the world, I guess."

Kedra was sure that Fruku would reveal their secret. "Right," she said, greatly relieved by his recovery.

"Certainly there's no shame in that," Lilliwan suggested. The twins nodded in agreement, hoping to avoid further questions without easy answers. "Listen, children," Lilliwan continued, "I need to run off to band practice."

"Again?" Fruku moaned.

"Again," Lilliwan confirmed. "But it's for a good cause, and anyway rehearsals will come to an end soon."

"Where is Dad?" wondered Kedra.

"He was called out to the dam on the Upper Throg," explained Lilliwan. "The mayor wanted to be sure that it can hold back the rain water. So you two will be on your own. I've left dinner in the oven. Be sure to get to bed by 9:00 if we're not home by then – you both look like you need a long rest." She then patted their damp heads and parted with the words that are compulsory for parents to say when leaving their children alone, but which in retrospect may seem foreboding: "And stay out of trouble."

"Don't worry," the twins promised. They had every good intention of following Lilliwan's orders, and for the first half hour tried to engage in perfectly normal activities. But, as could be expected, Jax lacked interest in moving from his spot on the rug, let alone in fetching anything. In her room Kedra sat in front of her dollhouse, at last deciding that further play would only lower her mood. Each glanced at a clock, finding that the time moved painfully slowly. Finally, whether due to events at the school, the outside gloom, or loneliness, Fruku uttered, "I'm bored."

"Me too," Kedra agreed. "But what shall we do?"

"I was thinking that we should take initiative."

"Oh," groaned Kedra. "You're not quoting 'Captain Luminous' again, are you?"

Her question hit a raw nerve. "What's strange about that?" demanded Fruku. "Anyway, if you want to be miserable, go ahead. As for me, I'd like to help Mom and Dad."

"How?"

"Well, Mom mentioned that she needs to clean. Maybe we can surprise her."

Kedra was not particularly enthused with the idea, but had nothing better to offer. "Fine," she agreed. "Maybe work is good for de-Wonkusing." The twins then set out in different directions, dusting this, polishing that, and finally rearranging furniture to sweep underneath.

"Kedra," Fruku called from the living room, "can you come here? The couch is too heavy to move by myself." With effort they managed to slide the piece forward."

"What's that," asked Kedra, pointing to a shiny object lying on the floor.

"A squeegee," Fruku declared confidently. He reached to picked up their find. "Jax must have carried it here," he continued, noting the teeth marks on the handle. "See?"

"Eww!" cried Kedra, recoiling at the thought of jiparix slobber. "You're not going to use it, are you?"

"Of course," Fruku proclaimed. "For scrubbing the walls."

"Isn't it time for bed?" Kedra suggested, hoping that their chores were already enough.

"If you do half and I do half we can finish quickly." Fruku then went for a rag and pail of water. He worked diligently, thoroughly wiping every surface, and managed the arced ceilings for good measure. "Your turn," he said to Kedra, handing over the squeegee and bucket.

Kedra also toiled swiftly and in silence. "Fruku?" she soon called from the final room. When he entered she asked, "What is this crackling sound?"

"I don't hear anything," he insisted.

"Listen closely. Can't you make anything out?"

"That's just the blade bending, I think," answered Fruku. And the conversation ended there. The twins, certain that their parents would be pleased with their resourcefulness, put everything back in place and dressed for bed.

While they were falling asleep Apseron finished his inspection of the dam. As he crossed Cobble Bridge he recalled that a certain invention, presumed to be ineffective, had gone missing. He resolved to find and bring it into working order.

Nearby, in his office, Mayor Tuggles remained in an ornery state. He intended to leave long ago, but having forgotten his umbrella stayed in the office late, hoping to wait out the rain. Consequently, Ms. Brumps felt obliged to remain at work. She had patiently endured hours of fussing and fretting.

"Blast that GubuGar," the mayor repeated for perhaps the hundredth time. "Unbearably indecisive and contradictory, they are. Shall I banish creatures with two heads?"

"I'm afraid that won't be possible, mayor," replied Ms. Brumps. "Just think of them as two voters in one."

"That's always been my policy!" chimed Gapron. "Nonetheless, they are a difficult lot. And do you know how they call themselves now?" Ms. Brumps was painfully aware of the title, but pretended otherwise. "Masters of Ceremonies. Which would be fine, except for the tiny fact that we are dangerously close not to having a ceremony! Because," he continued, still nervously walking back and forth, "we don't have a theme for Harvest Fest. And with their collective brains, what do you suppose they could dream up?" Again, the unflappable assistant feigned ignorance. "Let's hope there isn't snow. Snow!" he repeated, "in spring!"

"I suppose they were facing north at the time," offered Ms. Brumps, not knowing what else to say.

"Then we should all feel fortunate that they weren't looking east," complained the mayor. "Otherwise they should be warning of The Mudupan crashing the party."

Mayor Tuggles scrawled a few ideas of his own on a piece of paper. "Oh, toss it all," he cried, crumpling the top page and throwing it toward the bin. For better or worse, his eyes then fell on a sketch he made days ago. "Ms. Brumps, did I mention having my kitchen redone?" He had, of course, countless times, and the indifferent reaction conveyed as much. "What's strange about it?" Gapron wondered. "I bake an absolutely sumptuous Enchanted Forest Cake, you know."

"No doubt you do," replied the assistant, surreptitiously eyeing his considerable girth.

"Anyway, we're down to the final touches," Gapron continued. "Tell me, what is your opinion of this shape?" he asked, holding up an unconventional pattern.

Recognizing it to be (and there is no good way to put it delicately) the mark of a screechiwog smacking tail end into a wall, the long-suffering assistant hoped to exit the conversation quickly. "Well, to each his own, as they say. But as for me, I find it uninspiring, really."

"To the contrary," said Mayor Tuggles, "it's perfectly . . . what's the word? Daft?"

"You must have something else in mind," replied Ms. Brumps. "Daft is a put down."

"How's that?"

"You're then suggesting that it is," she paused, "silly, actually."

"Says who?" demanded Gapron.

"The dictionary."

"Well," huffed the mayor, "they should rewrite the dictionary, then. *I* say daft in a positive sense!"

"Mr. Mayor, people can't simply use words however they please."

"And why not?" demanded Gapron. "I find such rules highly constraining. If it suits me that *daft* is a compliment, who's to declare it shouldn't be so?"

"But think of the confusion," appealed Ms. Brumps. "What if everyone played with language that way?"

"Really," admonished the mayor, "don't be such a stick in the mud. A little more freedom would liven things up!"

"*Mess* things up, I'm afraid. It's a great benefit for meanings to be fixed."

"Is it, now? Such as?"

"Well, suppose that I tell you, 'Look at that lovely sunrise.' Only your understanding of *east* is what truly is *west*, so you would face the wrong way."

"Did you stop to think that I might not have planned to be up so early? That's very presumptuous! Maybe I want to sleep in, after all. You ought to be more careful with your examples."

"For the sake of argument," continued Ms. Brumps, by now seriously doubting the persuasive power of logic, "let's just say that you are wide awake."

"Whatever for?"

"It doesn't matter. Fine, let's say that you are deep in, um . . . important thoughts."

"Hm, I like the sound of that! Go on."

"You'd face the wrong direction," Ms. Brumps repeated.

The mayor blinked, otherwise showing no expression. "What's the harm in that?"

Ms. Brumps silently wondered whether something so obvious required explanation. "You'd miss the lovely sunrise, of course!"

"There I have you!" the mayor declared triumphantly. "I might see something even more interesting."

"Maybe," conceded Ms. Brumps, "but that's hardly the point! You would be standing with your back turned."

"I'll grant you that much, Ms. Brumps. But I fail to see the significance."

"For goodness sake, Mr. Mayor, how can anyone enjoy a sunrise looking the other way? How on earth could I have a conversation with your hind end?"

And at that Apseron's greatest fear was realized: Mayor Tuggles had, what he ambitiously labeled, a "Grand Idea."

～✺～

Back home, the twins were in their own reverie. Fruku dreamt that he was a knight in armor, fighting a baneful dragon. He feared not the thunder and lightning crashing about him, as they did in reality outside his bedroom. Both the beast and the very darkness trembled before his resplendent bravery as he drew his magic sword from the scabbard. How bright the kingdom was now! Kedra similarly pictured a castle, where in a dim tower she awaited rescue by a dashing prince. He approached, on a white steed. How radiantly they beckoned her! She prepared to leap to freedom as she heard a knock on the door. But the sound seemed eerily real. Then a voice called. "Kedra, are you sleeping?"

"I was," she replied. Her intonation bore the disappointment of having such a captivating scene spoiled. "What is it?"

The door opened quietly. "Do you remember the time we mopped the floors with blurpog oil?" Fruku whispered. He was referring to one of their father's more successful pursuits. The error, as they realized after the fact, was in storing the extract in an empty soap bottle. Consequently the members of the Sygard household (excepting their ever inert jiparix) slipped and slid around the home for the next week.

"Of course," Kedra winced. "Who can forget! That was an all-time low."

"So nothing could be worse, right?"

"Hardly. At least I wouldn't want to experience anything worse."

"Well, it's best not to open your eyes, then," Fruku suggested. "Good night."

But Wiggiwump nature being what it is, when one warns against an action the second can hardly resist taking it. And so Kedra rose, to find the house inexplicably pulsing with light. After overcoming the initial shock she slunk under her covers, hoping that if the problem didn't sort itself out by morning she would at least be sufficiently rested to cope with it. Fruku, withdrawn to his room, had come to the same conclusion.

CHAPTER 6

....

All that is Revealed after Rain

in which Fruku and Kedra receive both grief and reward,
experience a second improbable encounter, and wind down the day
with shadow play

"**F**ruku, are you awake?" Now it was Kedra's turn to ask. From the noises on the ground floor she knew that their parents were up and about. She supposed, correctly, that the shimmering shell of their home had disturbed their sleep, and preferred to face their certain annoyance together with her brother.

"Yes," came the terse reply. Fruku wished otherwise, but realized that they would need to offer an explanation sooner or later. And so he rose and joined his sister on the slow, contrite walk down the stairs.

The pleasant, familiar tones of the bariharp at first masked their timid footsteps. "Um, Mom and Dad," Kedra began as they reached the bottom.

"About the house glowing," continued Fruku when her voice trailed off, "we only wanted to help and, you see, we really didn't mean to . . ."

To their astonishment, they were spared an apology. "My geniuses!" proclaimed Apseron, rushing to embrace them. "Water," he continued as they exchanged confused glances, "that should have been plain all along! However did you know?"

"What?" was all that Kedra could think to say in response.

"Fruku, Kedra," Apseron continued, "don't you realize what this could mean?" Having not thought beyond the expected ridicule, the twins retained their vacant stares. "Why, dry lurdite is simply stone. But make it wet, give it a charge, and *presto*, there is light! True, anyone could have figured it out – in hindsight it's perfectly obvious – but in the end it was *your* discovery. So tell me, truly, how did you guess?"

Fruku also was at a loss. "Actually," he began, searching for the right words to confess to their dumb luck.

But again he was saved. "I might have known," Apseron ventured, smiling proudly. "The imaginations of children are positively miraculous. Whereas the minds of adults," he continued, tapping his head, "are filled with a good amount of clutter, which can stop us from seeing clearly. But the two of you aren't yet blinded by nonsense. That's the difference, without a doubt!"

"Yes, maybe," Kedra demurred, although in truth she felt that they had heard quite enough rubbish as of late.

"So you're not angry with us?" Fruku probed.

"Angry? Goodness, no. Granted, coming home to a glowing house gave your Mother a shock, but all turned out well."

"You're not mad at us either, Mom?" Kedra asked.

"I wasn't sure what to make of the situation at first," Lilliwan admitted. "But after your Father calmed me down I had an idea. Listen to this." As her fingers glided over the strings, the most majestic, uplifting of pieces filled the room. Even Jax stretched his ears to hear.

"That's beautiful!" Kedra proclaimed. "Is it something new?"

"Partially," Lilliwan answered. "I have been working on it for weeks, but wasn't inspired to finish two of the movements until last night. And would you like to know their titles?" she asked, grinning impishly. The twins eagerly nodded. "'Rain,' and 'Sun,' naturally!" Lilliwan went on to explain that the entire symphony was renamed "The Sky," and also covered clouds, wind, and snow. She would direct the public debut at the approaching Harvest Fest. There was just enough time to rehearse the newly completed parts. Now, all that remained was to find a bazziba player, for one musician had taken ill and the "Wind" movement in particular demanded the low notes unique to the largest of all horns.

The turn of events greatly unburdened the twins, who, having impatiently waited out the storm, yearned to go outside. Apseron stopped them momentarily. "We haven't yet spoken to the neighbors," he cautioned, "so be prepared for anything." He then returned to his lab, while Lilliwan resumed practicing "The Skies."

As they emerged it seemed that they had avoided scorn altogether. Not a soul walked the streets; in most homes the drapes were still drawn shut. Fruku carefully looked left and right, half expecting that they could not be let off so easily. Glancing upward, his stare then fell on an uninvited guest perched high on the roof. "Blast," he griped, "a screechiwog."

And then, for the second time that week, Fruku and Kedra were left with wide eyes and gaping mouths. "I don't want to be a bother," said the bird softly. "Be so kind to let me rest a few more minutes, and I will be on my way."

"You, you . . ." stammered Fruku.

"Spoke!" Kedra added, feeling feint. Now, it might be said in retrospect that the twins, with memories of meeting Eminalda fresh in their mind, should not have been caught utterly off guard. Yet no one supposed that there was such an animal as a pocket shrew, and consequently, it was never said that if such a creature lived, it ought not to talk. But a conversant screechiwog was on the whole something different.

This breed of fowl existed, as everyone knew, and it came in exactly one variety: non-talking. The idea that a screechiwog should make any sound other than ear-splitting shrieks was simply out of question. Thus Kedra and Fruku froze in place, gobsmacked, wondering if they should pinch themselves.

"And why not?" asked the guest calmly.

"But screechiwogs can't . . ." Fruku sputtered.

"Talk," filled in Kedra.

"That's usually for the better," the guest lamented. "Most have nothing worthwhile to contribute. In that case it's wise to stay silent. Don't you agree?" The twins nodded blankly. "And to be fair, it isn't so easy to talk while flying backward – that leaves a bird breathless, after all." The Screechiwog rose hesitantly off his perch. "Anyway, I've taken enough of your time."

"Wait," pleaded Kedra, by now slightly recovered. "At least tell us your name."

"Kiparu," the visitor shyly answered.

"I'm Fruku," came a steadying voice, "and this is my sister, Kedra."

"Pleased to meet you, Fruku and Kedra. It's been most hospitable of you to let me use your roof. I didn't mean to spend the night here; I must have been very tired after the storm. You can't imagine how scary that is, flying through dark rain clouds. I might have been lost entirely if not for a beacon, which turned out to be your house. Anyway, maybe I'll see you again," Kiparu intimated, preparing to take to the air. "Oh, sorry to ask, but would the two of you mind looking away a moment?"

"Can't you stay a little while longer?" Kedra entreated. "We've only just met, and we gave you a rude greeting. Please forgive us."

"It's simply that," continued Fruku, we aren't used to . . . ."

"A talking screechiwog," Kiparu finished the sentence, "I know. No need to apologize about that – the Cluster calls me a 'chattiwog.' That is," he corrected, "when we flock together, which is seldom. And when they do talk to me, which is even rarer. I think they mean to complain behind my back, actually, but being a forward flyer, and not yet a fast one, I usually catch slights right in the face. That hurt me at first. I've grown accustomed, though. Now, if you'll excuse me . . ."

"Please, just a moment," Fruku interjected, feeling his wits returning. "Do you not fly backwards?"

"Well, um, no," Kiparu answered bashfully. "Not any longer, that is."

"I could hardly believe it," Kedra volunteered, "at least not if I didn't already hear a screechiwog talk. Or do you prefer 'Chattiwog?'"

"As you wish," Kiparu replied. "One peculiarity is probably enough. I shouldn't have mentioned the second." The visitor then lowered his head.

"Why not?" Fruku wondered.

"Because, to be honest, I am still a little self-conscious. It's not easy to go against the Cluster, you know. They insist that I'm simply difficult, that I want to be unlike them, as if that is shameful. But one day it occurred to me that there might be a better way to fly, and so I tried to go head first."

Fruku, ever the rescuer of failed attempts, related to this point. "And it worked, didn't it!"

"Not entirely," the Chattiwog (now accepted as such) admitted. "It's difficult to break old habits. And there was no one to teach me; I needed to learn on my own. The others didn't want to fly with me, especially in the beginning, because I kept knocking them sideways. Still, it's a great advantage to see where I want to go – tail feathers are much better trailing than covering the eyes, I can promise you. Now I mostly manage a straight line. At times I even think that the rest might follow after me some day. But there is much work to do." Kiparu's neck then stiffened. "Pardon me, Kedra and Fruku, it's been a pleasure, but I really need to go – someone is coming."

"Will we see you again?" Kedra wondered.

"Nothing happens by accident," answered the Chattiwog. "If we are meant to meet, we will." And he disappeared, almost as discretely as he had arrived.

No sooner had the Chattiwog flown off when Fruku, spotting a certain classmate approaching, whispered all of one word to Kedra: "Druzina."

Nothing more needed to be said. "Quick," she ventured, "let's go inside before she spots us."

Unfortunately the suggestion came too late. "Hello, *Fruku*. Hello, *Kedra*." As children often do, Druzina stressed their names as if they were, of themselves, insults.

"Hi, Druzina," Fruku replied unenthusiastically.

"I'm ever so glad to know that the two of you are safe." *Goodness*, Kedra thought, *she's even more two-faced than GubuGar*. "I was out taking a walk earlier this morning – I like to do that, you know; fresh air is very good for my complexion – when I saw a terrible light shooting up from your neighborhood. You can hardly imagine how concerned I was. And," she continued in the tone of someone delighting in nabbing a foe red handed, "as we all can see, it's coming from *your roof*."

"It's nothing," Fruku assured. "In a few hours everything should be back to normal."

"And I'm so glad of that! As I said, I came over simply to put my mind at ease." Meanwhile Kedra shot a futile glance toward Jax, who, being asleep on the threshold, could not heed her silent command to attack.

"We'll, you're safe, and that's the most important thing. I really did have a horrible shortness of breath thinking that you might not be," she claimed, carefully placing a hand on her most precious heart. "Anyway," she added, casting pleasantries aside, "now we can all agree that this glowing roof is really a desperate call for attention, don't you think?"

"So leave if it bothers you," Fruku shot back. *Kill, kill!* Kedra thought, trying to will a telepathic connection with the jiparix into place.

"Look," Druzina replied, feigning offense, "I didn't say that *I* find it desperate. I'm trying to support you. But, as a teeny bit of friendly advice, you have to be realistic – a glowing roof simply screams out to be noticed. After all, cultured Wiggiwumps have the decency not to disturb the peace like that. Why, I can hardly think of anything so hopeless."

"I can," Kedra retorted, now directing her annoyed stare squarely at the unwelcome visitor.

"My dear *Kedra*," Druzina continued, "Don't get me wrong. You can count on me not to say anything about this embarrassment of yours. My lips are sealed. Of course," she grinned, "by now the whole village probably knows, as painfully obvious as the situation is. So please, when you hear the whole school laughing at you, know that your friend Druzina hasn't breathed a word to anyone."

And at that, before either of the twins could come up with a suitable reply, she turned around and left, swishing from side to side with malicious glee. Fruku then took a turn gazing disapprovingly at Jax, wishing that his jiparix were like Highgloss and would pounce on her from behind.

No sooner had Druzina left when they heard a vaguely familiar voice. "That was quite a show last night." The twins were dismayed to find Mr. Makiloyd standing behind them, and braced for a lecture. "Living next to your Father all these years, by now nothing should surprise me," he continued. "But a whole house lighting up . . ." His words trailed off in a whistle. "I suppose no one in the neighborhood had a good night's sleep."

"It wasn't Dad this time," admitted Fruku. "At least not entirely. You see," he started, "Father was in his laboratory, working on an experiment, and it might have worked, except that he was distracted, and . . . ." Realizing that the predicament bore no easy explanation he broke off the attempt.

"Let me guess," filled in Mr. Makiloyd. "This has something to do with another flop."

"It's not a flop!" Fruku insisted. "It's simply a case of, well, things not going according to the plan."

Kedra hoped to put the conversation on a more favorable path. "We were only trying to help," she offered.

"Yes," Fruku agreed. "We wanted to show initiative. You see, we were watching 'Captain Luminous,' and . . . ." Kedra shot her brother a reproachful look, as if to ask, *Why did you have to mention that?*

But Mr. Makiloyd's tone became reflective. "That's something from my younger years," he said, stroking his chin. "I didn't know anyone still watches the show."

"No one except Fruku," Kedra added. "And I, sometimes," she admitted.

"Just a moment, kids, I might have something for you." After a minute Mr. Makiloyd returned with a tattered book. "You'll have to be careful with this," he said, handing it to them.

Fruku could hardly believe his eyes, for he was holding a rare copy of "The Heroic Tales of Captain Luminous." "This is out of print," he exclaimed. "Not even Aunt Vreena could find it for a hundred Bracks. I don't know what to say, Mr. Makiloyd," Fruku continued. "Except for thank you, of course."

"Enjoy," said Mr. Makiloyd, flashing a trace of a smile. "Oh, and don't worry too much about the house. Trying and not succeeding is forgivable. The only real failure in life is not to take chances."

The twins nodded in amazement. As they took their gift inside the Sygard home had already faded back into normality. On her way out to rehearsal, Lilliwan smiled at them, also certain that all was well.

~)(~)

But the solace was short lived, for the nose of an all-too-familiar interloper soon poked through the open door. "Hello, the house!" squealed Gar, having inserted his head to survey the room.

Not again, thought Apseron, who was working diligently on a new prototype, a distance whisperer as it happened to be. Jax, as usual, shirked his guard duty and paid no attention either to GubuGar or the disappointed stare of his master. "And what can I do for you today?" Apseron asked politely.

"You might inquire what *we* can do for *you*," corrected Gubu.

"We come bearing an invitation," Gar added with an air of officialdom. But having flippers they could not hand it over and thus requested Apseron to detach an embossed envelope from what seemed to be a uniform.

"Gapron Tuggles, Mayor of Wiggiwump Village, requests the honor of the company of Apseron Sygard at the annual Harvest Fest," the inventor read aloud. "Guests are kindly reminded to dress in keeping with the dignity of the theme, 'THINKING BACKWARDS.'"

"Shall we inform the mayor of your acceptance?" Gubu asked.

Apseron, having little fondness for ceremonies in general and this one in particular, searched for a polite way to decline. "Please tell the mayor that, regrettably, I would be unable to go without Lilliwan."

"Oh, she is invited," Gar assured him.

Gubu added, "as the band director, that goes without saying."

"But I need permission to attend?"

The two heads nodded in confirmation. "You'll need to sit by yourself," Gubu explained. "Lilliwan is a VIP." "Very important person," Gar added, "like us."

Apseron understood that he had no escape, resented having to say so to GubuGar, and on top of it all found the riotous pattern of their attire nauseating. "What, exactly, is that design on your outfit?"

GubuGar proudly thrust out their collective chest. "Why, nothing less than screechiwog rump, of course!" Gubu proudly declared.

"Tailor-made for us, the new village couriers," Gar added, "and what's more, it's in mode."

Apserson found both the visitors and their conclusion preposterous. "I suppose you are authorities on style now."

"Naturally," Gubu replied. "We are not only the Factotum of the Glen, but fashionisti too!"

"Well, I am, anyway," Gar clarified. Being eyeless, he did not notice Gubu jealously squinting at him.

"Do you mean to tell me that you will be dressed this way for the festival?"

"Of course," Gubu boomed. "Screechiwog rump is the new black."

The conversation had become too much for the highly rational mind of Apseron. "Surely you are joking!"

"And what is *he* wearing," Gar haughtily inquired of Gubu.

"A scientist's robe. Cream colored, to be precise."

"Meaning, the *old* black," Gar replied dismissively.

"Oh no, that simply will not do. We advise you to follow our lead."

"Come," said the Gar to the Gubu head, "let us take our leave." And off they waddled with their shared nose held high. Watching them slide away, Apseron wondered if he might not be able to invent GubuGar repellent.

∽ᗡᑑᗧᑋᓚ

On the walk to the band hall Lilliwan chanced across Rispard, who, as usual, looked like he was up to no good. When he noticed her he quickly hid something in his pocket and grinned sheepishly. "Rispard, what's that?" Lilliwan demanded.

"What?" he replied, pretending not to understand the question. But Lilliwan was well versed in the ways of twelve-year olds and gave him her best *you can't fool me* stare. Slowly he withdrew his hand. She looked at the rock he clenched, then at the stained glass window that most certainly was the target, and finally directly into his eyes. Rispard lowered his shoulders, and, to his own surprise, dropped the stone onto the ground.

"Rispard," she said, "there are a few troublemakers in this village. But I don't believe that you're one of them. Or at least, you don't want to be. So tell me, why were you about to break that glass?"

"I wasn't," he started to insist. Then, realizing that there was little point to arguing, admitted, "I don't know, actually."

"I'll tell you why," Lilliwan declared. "Because you want to be noticed, but are not sure how. Am I right?"

Rispard was not used to anyone talking to him in this manner, and felt himself flushing crimson. "Maybe," he agreed, quivering slightly.

"Listen," Lilliwan continued. "Have you ever taken music lessons?"

"No," he replied. "I haven't tried much of anything."

"That doesn't matter. There is always a first time." As Mothers are able, her intonation then became at once a question and a statement. "Why don't you join the brass band?"

Such a thought had never occurred to Rispard. "But what if I have no talent for music?"

"And what if you do?" Lilliwan returned, motioning toward the hall.

The conversation pricked at an insecure spot that Rispard had long hidden from himself. "Thanks, Ms. Sygard, but I really doubt that I can manage."

"Try this," replied Lilliwan. "Make your best *bah!* sound, at the top of your lungs."

Rispard was accustomed to being told to keep his voice down. Permission to shout was something special indeed! "BAAHHHH!!!" he bellowed, shaking the very glass that he nearly shattered earlier with a stone.

"That's perfect!" Lilliwan confirmed. "If you can't play the bazziba, I don't know who can."

"Well, I'm still not sure," he said, though secretly he might have wished otherwise.

Lilliwan shifted tactics. "I understand," she assured him. "The bazziba is powerful, like the wind. Why, even to hold it upright demands a strong person."

"But I'm strong!" Rispard protested, forgetting his initial reluctance. And with this cunning ploy the band was again complete.

The day, and for that matter, the week, had been one of the most momentous in recollection – scarcely could the twins imagine further oddities. Consequently, as the sun set over the Glen that evening they felt a need to reflect on recent events. And so, as they often did when they wished to be alone with their thoughts, they sought refuge in their twine house.

Their parents had finished this magnificent sanctuary four springs ago. A jinjibar in their back yard was still growing at the time. Apseron, envisioning a structure that could adapt along with the host tree, hit upon the use of stretch rope. Lilliwan carefully arranged the cords from branch to root in a configuration that made a rough hyperboloid, as the twins learned it to be. Suspended in the middle was an enclosed orb, into which the troubles of the adult world seldom intruded.

The twins quickly ascended the side ladder. The interior darkened when they closed the side flap behind them. Accordingly Fruku reached for a lamp, one of the few possessions kept inside. "Here," Fruku said, passing the light to his sister, "shine this against the wall."

"What's that," Kedra wondered. Fruku had put his hands together, one in the shape of a fist and the other with fingers fanned out. It was not yet clear which silhouette he meant to create. He then enhanced one part, altered another, throwing a more familiar shadow.

"It's a screechiwog," Kedra cried. "Or a chattiwog, actually," she added, noting the direction of flight. "Fruku," she continued, "it's as if I am reliving a dream. Is Kiparu real? And does he truly talk, or did I only imagine him?"

"He's real," Fruku affirmed, "and yes, unless I also was dreaming, we actually had a conversation with him."

"My turn," Kedra continued, giving the lamp to her brother. "Do you know what I can't understand?"

"No," Fruku admitted.

"Why us? I mean, such things simply don't happen in the Glen. Or they didn't, anyway." Kedra paused briefly to cast her own figure. "Lately they not only happen, but to you and me. Why do you suppose that is? We're ordinary, aren't we?"

"Eminalda!" said Fruku, reacting to the shape on the wall. "That was easy. And maybe not. Anyway, what's the fun of being ordinary? Here, take the light."

"Look, I'm not suggesting that we're exactly like the rest. But are we so different that shrews and screechiwogs should talk to us, and to no one else?"

Fruku was half engaged with forming an object, large but as yet nondescript, on the wall. "Maybe they made a wise choice," he casually replied. "Suppose that Kiparu tried to start a conversation from Mr. Mramsee's roof."

The thought made Kedra giggle. "Mr. Mramsee would have fainted straight away!" she replied.

"So you see, there would have been no point. Can you tell what this is?"

"A jumping jiparix?"

Fruku winced. "Actually, I'm trying to picture how The Mudupan would look."

"Well," offered Kedra, "make it much scarier."

Fruku put his wrists together, opening and closing his spread fingers. The shadow indeed resembled gnashing jaws with sharp teeth. "And now?"

"That's better," Kedra agreed. Then, realizing that the hour was late, the twins exchanged the twine house for their bedrooms. While drifting off to sleep, each wished that troubles were as fleeting as the shadows that had dissipated in their fort.

CHAPTER 7

The Worst Fear
Comes to Pass

*in which Apseron and Lilliwan separately relate
to Wonkus, the twins commit an act of kindness,
and consequently they receive alarming news*

s the sun arced over the Glen several mornings later the residents eagerly took to the streets – at last, Harvest Fest had arrived. For not merely weeks but months, going back to the prior, lengthening autumn nights and first flakes of snow, through the long, cold winter and subsequent return of the screechiwogs and spring rains, they had waited for this happy occasion. And thus, with the start of the celebration still hours off, they already rose to greet neighbors, to iron their favorite clothes, to primp and preen, and otherwise to prepare for the greatest fête of the year.

By all accounts it would be one of the finest in recollection. Mayor Tuggles, now thoroughly confident in the program (save for a final touch or two still to be made) had pledged no less, and additionally hinted at unforgettable surprises. For children the event was not only a wonder in itself but a passage into summer, which for Kedra and Fruku meant spending carefree weeks with their maternal grandparents in the countryside. Not least of all, the yield of the brackawack, the very cause for celebration, had been particularly bountiful this season. In short, moods were high, and the day admitted of no break in merriment.

Yet even at this moment of boundless promise, Jax would not deign to alert the Sygards to visitors. Nor could Lilliwan, seated at her bariharp in deep concentration, detect the unexpected footsteps over the captivating melody issuing forth. And so the expectant face of Mayor Tuggles breached their threshold unheard.

"Well, I must say," bellowed Gapron, "that is simply splendid!"

"Oh, it's you," exclaimed Lilliwan with mild apprehension.

"And who else!" declared the guest, now fully inside. "The big day is upon us, after all, and there could hardly be a Harvest Fest without music! So I thought that a courtesy call to our esteemed conductor was in order." His tone then became more business-like. "Are we on task?" he tersely inquired. By *we*, Lilliwan correctly understood that the mayor referred to *her*, and for her part she had not anticipated any obstacle to the upcoming performance. "Say," Gapron continued, "which song were you playing just now?"

That the mayor should need an answer to this question gave Lilliwan a sense of unease. "It's 'The Wind,'" she replied, "from the symphony that our band will premiere this evening."

"Of course it is," Gapron affirmed, as if he were aware all along. "Be so kind as to remind me of the name."

"The Skies," Lilliwan answered with aplomb.

Gapron seemed wholly unmoved. "Hm," he responded, stroking his chin. "That's a bit high-minded, don't you think?"

Lilliwan managed to suppress disdain. "Well, yes, that's exactly what skies are." The mayor returned only a blank stare, and so she added, for clarity, "a source of inspiration."

"Naturally," he tepidly agreed.

"But?" Lilliwan prompted, surmising that the mayor had not yet come to the essence.

"But . . ." continued Gapron, "is inspiration really what we want?"

Lilliwan understood that *we* now meant *everyone except her*. She had long labored over the composition, correcting errant notes, removing unneeded measures, and bringing the whole into a stirring unity. "Gapron," she unceremoniously declared, "I have written a symphony, not a referendum. 'The Skies' is meant to lift up the audience."

"That is a great relief indeed," replied the mayor. "Forgive me," he continued, laughing. "For a moment I worried that you expected contemplation." The last word he pronounced as if it were odious.

"Of course I do!" Lilliwan corrected him. "That's the very point! The music should move listeners to reflect on something vast, on the transcendent. Like most artists I want to provoke a sense of awe."

Now the mayor became unnerved. "Lilliwan," he implored, "with all due respect for your noble ideals, practically speaking there is thinking, and there is feeling. And it's better that the two not mix, especially on a day when the public craves entertainment."

"Is that what you believe," cried Lilliwan, "that they want empty fun, and nothing more?"

"Exactly," the mayor affirmed, supposing that they had found common ground.

Lilliwan had quite another understanding of the situation. "Are you suggesting that I not play the music?" she asked with evident irritation.

"Oh, goodness, no," the mayor assured her. "But perhaps it should be, a little bit . . . what's the word? Diluted."

Lilliwan was aghast. "Diluted!?"

"Or maybe played a bit faster. Presently it's rather dour, isn't it? But fortunately that's a quick fix," he decided. "Simply waive your baton more emphatically – that's how it's done, isn't it? – and it will be a smash! Yes, that's the solution – I can picture everyone wiggling with joy."

Lilliwan was now fully steamed. "Listen carefully," she warned. "I will not change the tempo simply to suit your fancy. Nor will I drop out a single note, or conduct the movements louder or softer than intended. The music will stay as it needs to be to convey the right emotions! Am I clear?"

This candor caught the mayor entirely off guard. "You're right, no doubt," he muttered, nervously clutching at his tie. "We will simply change the name, then."

"That is also non-negotiable!" Lilliwan insisted.

"Well," stammered the mayor, "I'm afraid that a different title is already printed."

"And what is that?" demanded Lilliwan, mortified by this misappropriation.

"Something more down to earth and in line with the theme this year," replied the mayor. "'A New Way of Walking.'" And before Lilliwan could express her displeasure, he made his exit. Speechless, she looked to the heavens, hoping for a restoration of sanity.

Apseron, on his way to the town center, was about to suffer his own tribulations. He was already out of sorts, having been requested to examine the VIP stand, on which, apparently, he was insufficiently important to sit during the actual event. While approaching the belfry he heard a voice from behind. "Mr. Sygard, is that you?"

"Ah, Principal Priggins," he returned, half regretting that he was not already out of earshot.

"It's good that we met. I've been hoping to run into you."

Why is that? he wondered. Taking note of the principal's imperious stare and recalling the twins' subdued demeanors of late, he correctly guessed the purpose for seeking him out. "Has there been a problem at school?"

"Oh, I wouldn't call it a problem as such," she addressed him, "but only a need for a minor correction. You see, we value individualism highly – that goes without saying." Apseron kept silent and returned a stare that communicated, *Well, go on.*

"And," she continued after a brief pause, "your kids certainly stand apart!"

"Thank you," Apseron replied, accepting this fact in a positive light. "They are indeed dynamic children. Lilliwan and I are very proud of them," he stressed.

"As well you should be. And so are we, naturally," assured the Principal, belying a different motive. "They're certainly full of surprises, to say the least. Why, are you aware that lately they've been discussing a talking rat – a pharmacist, I think – a forward-flying screechiwog, and, if I'm not mistaken a glowing roof." She laughed while probing for a sign of concern.

"That doesn't surprise me," Apseron responded calmly. "We encourage development of their imaginations."

"Quite right, quite right," the Principal replied. "To a point, that is. These things always need to be moderated, don't they. Do you follow?" she asked.

"I'm not sure, Ms. Priggins. What exactly do you mean?"

"Well, Mr. Sygard. To put it frankly, and please don't take offense, your children have been, shall we say, disruptive."

"How so?" Apseron replied. "Is it a question of discipline in the classroom?"

"Well, in a manner of speaking, yes. At least indirectly. You see, they have a tendency to misuse their intellects."

Apseron silently recalled that the twins had referred to Humberbred as a blundering drivel-spewing ignoramus (or words to that effect), and Druzina as a spoiled, whiny, energy parasite (to paraphrase), and wondered what they might have said at school. "Are they putting down the other students?" he wondered.

"Yes, I'm afraid so. Somewhat," she partially backtracked. "They might not consciously intend to, to be fair, but in comparison their classmates feel inadequate at times. That is out of step with our philosophy, which is that every child should be average or above."

"For my better understanding, in which category are Kedra and Fruku."

"Average or above!"

"And you're suggesting that when they apply themselves . . ."

"Children who might doubt that they are average or above . . ." the Principal interrupted.

"Of which there are none," Apseron filled in.

"Exactly," Principal Priggins affirmed, pleased to be getting her point across. "Those children, whom we certainly hope are not found in the classroom, may become insecure when their peers shine too brightly. I'm afraid that we've had a few complaints to this effect."

So you mean to say that my children should hold themselves back."

"Well, Mr. Sygard, that's put a little too bluntly, though broadly stated, it's more or less what we had in mind," the Principal confirmed. "Can I then count on you to have a delicate word with your kids?"

"Just to clarify, you want me to tell my children not to stand out?"

"That's not entirely what we ask," the Principal qualified. "As I said in the beginning, we encourage individualism! But perhaps we can explore other ways for your children to distinguish themselves. For example, a slightly rebellious shirt for Fruku. Or pig tails for Kedra."

"Pig tails!" Apseron repeated with alarm.

"Perhaps a bunt, then?" Ms. Priggins offered.

"Do you mean to tell me that my children, in place of developing their talents fully, are expected to channel their energy into *appearing* to be different!?"

"Please understand my predicament, Mr. Sygard, it's much easier for us to overlook that kind of expressiveness."

Apseron, having heard quite enough, was no longer able to restrain himself. "I'll do no such thing! Listen carefully, Ms. Priggins, my children will not be advised to underperform. If others feel left behind, your time would be put to much better use raising their expectations." And with that he promptly declared an end to the conversation and excused himself.

Well, the Principal thought, *I always viewed Lilliwan as a firebrand, but I can see that the twins get their verve from both sides.*

By late afternoon Kedra and Fruku grew impatient for the start of Harvest Fest. After playing several rounds of Silly Questions, trying in vain to provoke Jax into action, and even putting their rooms in order, it seemed that they had exhausted all options for passing the remaining hours. At last Fruku suggested that they pay a visit to Eminalda.

"Mom, we'll be out for a little while," Kedra yelled from the bottom of the stairs.

Lilliwan was then in the kitchen, still smarting over the profanation of her symphony. "Where are you going?" she called after them.

"To the forest," replied Fruku. Taking their Mother's silence as a cue to say more, and realizing that they could not disclose their intention, he offered a partial truth. "I lost my oddball there, and want to find it."

"Just don't be late this evening," Lilliwan replied. "The music will start at 8:00 pm sharp."

"Yes, Mom," the twins agreed in unison. Through the window, Lilliwan noticed that they were carrying a small sack, and wondered why it should be necessary.

The walk indeed calmed the twins, and as they passed beyond the last of the village houses they forgot about the time altogether. Happy and relaxed, it no longer struck them as strange that they would soon resume a conversation with a talking shrew. "Eminalda?" Kedra called softly as they approached the knotty jinjibar.

"Who's there?" returned the familiar voice.

"It's us, Fruku and Kedra."

"Hold your fire, please," added Fruku, recalling the previous pelting.

"Just a moment, children, while I make myself presentable." Shortly after Eminalda scurried up from the inside. "What do you think?" she asked, pointing to a bonnet delicately arranged on her head.

There can only be one correct reply to such a question, as any well-bred girl knows. "You look lovely," Kedra replied.

"Well, of course I do!" declared Eminalda. "That's the point, you know. A lady wants to look her best when she receives guests, even if she's round about 331, and cantankerous to boot."

"We've brought you something. Haven't we, Kedra?" Fruku prompted, nudging his sister in the side.

"Yes," Kedra reluctantly agreed. "We thought that these might be useful for your new home." She reached into the pouch, first pulling out a miniature table.

"Absolutely perfect!" Eminalda joyfully exclaimed. "Why, it's everything I need. That is," she continued, "unless you happen to have a few stools to go with it." Kedra nodded and retrieved matching chairs. "We'll, that's simply divine of you. The set makes my kitchen complete.

Though . . ." her voice trailed off, "I can't help noticing that your grab bag is not quite empty."

"We brought you a ladder, too," grinned Fruku.

"That's smashing, and just the right height. Moreover, it will be much easier for me to carry down the table and chairs. And," she emphasized, waving a tiny paw toward a bulge in the sack, "whatever else might still be lying in the bottom there."

Kedra hesitatingly obliged. "You can hang your hat on this," she said, pulling out a coat rack. "And, finally, here is a cabinet, for your herbs."

"Marvelous, children," squealed Eminalda. "And all in milky white, my seventh favorite color!"

"It will go nicely with your eggball," Kedra suggested, taking satisfaction in watching Fruku wince in return.

"Well, it would. Except that I've made a few improvements. If you don't mind putting the ladder in place I'll show you." Eminalda then gleefully descended her new steps and, moaning and grunting, managed to lift up the oddball, now painted orangey-brown. Atop she had sketched a most unpleasant face. "What do you think?"

Fruku grimaced at the thought of changes to his favorite toy. "It looks like The Mudupan," Kedra replied.

"How enormously clever you are!" confirmed Eminalda. "You can hardly imagine how much more I enjoy bashing it now."

"Why is that?" Fruku prompted.

"Why indeed!" huffed Eminalda. "As if you wouldn't like to do the same if The Mudupan crushed *your* house."

"What!?" cried the twins in joint alarm.

The shrew in turn found their reactions surprising. "Heaven sakes," she replied, "don't go wobbly kneed on me! Anyway, had I not mentioned that detail earlier?" Kedra and Fruku simply shook their heads. "I certainly meant to," Eminalda continued. "Well, when you reach 326, give or take a few years, a thought might occasionally slip your mind too."

"But The Mudupan is just an old wives' tale," Fruku said, hoping that to be the case.

"Is it now! Next I suppose you'll claim not to believe in talking shrews either. A fat lot of good that does, by the way, to know that my beautiful home was trampled by an imaginary creature. I feel consoled, thank you very much. As for this old wife," she said, thumping her chest, "at least I would be, if there were a man brave enough to take me as his bride, I can point you to a very real hoof print or two that shows otherwise."

"That explains why you came here," Kedra empathized.

"Of course it does. Heavens, do you think I'm in the habit of moving into tree holes willy-nilly? I had a perfectly suitable manse, with a library, fireplace, and even a drawing room, where every six or seven years I entertained guests. That is, until a foul-tempered, heartless, smelly, no-account brute stomped on it."

"How horrible," Kedra said, aghast.

"Well, at least I don't take it personally any more. I suppose The Mudupan was simply out prowling. Thankfully, so was *I* at the time. But that certainly was a fine welcome when I came home. Or to what little was left of it, anyway."

"We need to tell Mom and Dad," Fruku said. "They'll know what to do."

"Yes, children, you'd better give warning." And with that the twins sprinted away. "Oh, one last thing," Eminalda cried after them. "I'm afraid I couldn't find anything to help with your Wonkus."

As was often their misfortune, on their return the twins encountered GubuGar. On this occasion they were beside the path, lazing in a mud hole, rubbing themselves and singing a duet out of tune. "Bipeddy boppety BOOOOO," they chimed. "Bubba Babba BOWWWW." Such a spectacle would leave most passersby grasping for words, and thus Fruku can easily be forgiven for mustering nothing better than, "What are you doing?"

"We're loafing," Gar candidly replied.

"Having a bath, if you please," Gubu corrected. Pursing his lips, he made *puk puk puk* sounds, like soap bubbles popping.

"That's what we meant," Gar agreed. "We're purifying ourselves."

"Before the big event," Gubu added. "We want our skin to be lusciously smooth, baby-skin soft."

"Quite irresistibly, huggably kissable!" finished Gar. Kedra, recalling the recent game of Silly Questions, shuddered.

Fruku had neither the time nor the stomach for further conversation. "I don't suppose you know the path between here and Tryg Mountain."

"Naturally," Gar squealed in reply. "As the Factotum of the Glen we are first-rate cartographers."

"Among a plethora of talents," Gubu added.

"Then tell me," said Fruku, "how would The Mudupan attack Wiggiwump Village? By the . . ." But he could not finish his question, for at the mention of the beast, GubuGar dove into the mud, leaving only a quivering nose protruding. After some time an ear and mouth, both of unknown origin, cautiously poked above the surface. "All clear?" came a trembling voice from one or the other head.

Kedra decided against the sympathetic approach. "Look," she demanded, "we don't have time for silliness! And though it pains me to say it, we need your help. So pull yourselves together – right now!" On her order GubuGar crept timidly from the mud pool.

"Once again," Fruku demanded, "and try to think clearly. Which way will The Mudupan come?"

Gar tried his best to look contemplative. "Hm," he said. "I suppose it would fly."

"Yes," Gubu pensively agreed. "A beeline would be most sensible."

"Except," Kedra yelled, "it has no wings!"

"And why should *you* decide who flies and who doesn't?" Gubu inquired. "That hardly seems fair. Why, we ourselves would so enjoy soaring like an eagle!" GubuGar, swooning over the majestic vision, rolled side to side. Imagining a dramatic aerial roll to the right, the bulbous frame fell, Gubu-head first. The twins jumped back, barely avoiding the splashing. Fortunately, the crash also brought GubuGar back to earth in a literal sense. "I suppose that is a valid point," Gar admitted. "We are then left with two possibilities."

"I think he'll go that way," Gubu said, pointing to the west.

"Stuff and nonsense," Gar contradicted. "Wipe your eyeball before you direct us anywhere."

"I mean, *that* way," Gubu corrected himself, having made a cumbersome turn to the southeast. "Through the Enchanted Forest."

"Some cartographer you are," Gar chided. "It would certainly attack by the Gronk Narrows." Gar then shook a flipper imprecisely to the northeast.

"I don't agree with your conclusion," Gubu protested. "Let's put this to a vote!"

"Fine," Gar conceded. "All in favor of the Gronk Narrows, say aye. Aye! And all opposed, nay."

"Nay!" Gubu shouted.

"Blast," bemoaned Gar, "another tie."

"Look," proposed Gubu. "For the sake of consensus, if you go with the Enchanted Forest I will let you be King for a day."

"Why didn't you say so straight away," Gar replied. "The Enchanted Forest it is!"

Kedra and Fruku, having abandoned hope of extracting useful information, were by then nearly out of earshot. The harmony was short lived in any event, for Gubu and Gar started quarreling over the limits of kingly authority and whether a "day" meant 24 hours or only the span from sunrise to sunset. The second of these quibbles in turn reminded them that time was running short. Hence they forgot the previous conversation entirely and resumed the spa treatment before their presentation at Harvest Fest. Meanwhile the twins pressed on, unsure of what fate held in store for them.

CHAPTER 8

A Courageous Stand

in which the twins, with the aid of friends,
cunning, and pluck, prove their mettle

The Mudupan – in flesh and blood, and not merely the stuff of legends – was at that very moment stoking a fire inside its cave. It had just returned from a walk, gathering a final load of wood that lay in a pile beside. The beast greedily smacked its lips in anticipation of the roast, to consist of Wiggiwumps, fatted on brackawack berries, rotated on a makeshift spit.

The emerging smoke went unnoticed, save for a forward-flying screechiwog fortuitously passing by just then. Kiparu knew that something was amiss. Wondering whom he might warn, he could only think of the kind boy and girl on whose glowing roof he had taken refuge. And so he turned back toward Wiggiwump Village, hoping to find the twins at home.

Kedra and Fruku were halfway back when they heard a vaguely familiar voice call their names. Looking futilely around them they realized that the cry came from above. "Incoming!" Kiparu warned, not yet fully confident in his front-facing approach. The Chattiwog touched down on his claws, timidly but without any of the bumps or rolls that characterized prior attempts.

It was clear that he had flown with an urgency of purpose. "I'm glad to find you," Kiparu said, after regaining his breath. "The Mudupan is on the loose."

"We know," Fruku replied. "We are off to tell the village."

"There won't be time for that," warned Kiparu. "It is already on the way, and judging by the pace, will get there first."

"What shall we do?" Kedra asked nervously.

Fruku knew the answer, though it gave little comfort. "We need to stop it first."

"Agreed!" affirmed the Chattiwog, whose enthusiasm then dampened. "Of course, that's easier said than done."

A brief silence fell over the three. "What do we know about the situation?" Fruku at last asked. "According to GubuGar, it will attack either by the Enchanted Forest or Gronk Narrows."

"I already don't like the sound of this," protested Kedra, reacting to the notion of relying on advice from GubuGar.

"Those are the two likely choices," Kiparu suggested. "But which?"

"Let's go back to the Enchanted Forest," suggested Fruku.

"Wait," Kedra interjected. "That's what GubuGar guessed." The others stared blankly, not following the logic. "So," she explained, "considering the source, in all likelihood The Mudupan will come through Gronk Narrows."

"You might be onto something there," Fruku concurred. "But Eminalda is in the forest. We need to warn her. And she might know what to do in any case."

"Who is Eminalda?" Kiparu wondered.

"Our friend," Kedra explained. "She is a 300-year old pocket shrew who lives in a tree and mixes herbs. She is going to cure our Wonkus. Oh, and beware: she is very gabby." Now, as is understood only with age, some truths are better administered by the drop. Upon seeing the confused expression of the Chattiwog, Kedra realized that such a torrent might not have been advisable.

Kiparu blinked slowly while considering this information. "Pardon the question," he said at last, "but simply to know what I am getting myself into, is this friend of yours real?"

"Of course!" Kedra insisted, in the miffed tone of a girl being doubted.

"A talking mouse?" Kiparu stressed, inviting reconfirmation.

"Shrew," Fruku corrected. "She is very touchy about that."

"And what's strange about it?" Kedra demanded. "You are a talking screechiwog, after all."

"Point taken," conceded Kiparu. "But the three of us, plus a rodent, are hardly a match for The Mudupan."

"Anyone with a better idea, speak up!" Fruku challenged. The trio had to admit that a slim chance was better than none at all. And so Kedra and Fruku retraced their steps, with Kiparu following closely behind. They passed the now vacant mud bath and pressed on to the grove. Each was nervous and, to be sure, more than once bemoaned the burden of responsibility.

They didn't have GubuGar specifically in mind at that moment, though the discontent would well have applied. Fresh from the mud bath (or as clean as a GubuGar can be, anyway) and dressed in their finest (to the extent it is possible), they were at that moment lumbering on to the celebration.

"Today is our day!" Gubu uttered with delight.

"Nothing can stand in our way!" Gar echoed.

"Say," asked, Gubu, "what's that?" Nearby was a familiar bush. Now, if there is anything GubuGars love more than the berries of the brackawack in general, it is only the low-hanging variety. And this particular bush, which had, as if by miracle, not been picked clean, offered something better still: a juicy yield already dropped to the ground, requiring no plucking.

"Hoorah!" Gar cried. "It's almost too good to be true." Then, detecting a pungent waft, he inquired, "Do you suppose they are rotten?"

Gubu was not in a mindset to let such a triviality ruin the good fortune. "No, I think not."

"Your opinion on this topic would count for considerably more," noted Gar, "if you had a nose."

Gubu might have argued had his mouth not already been full. "They taste fine to me," he at last managed to say, between eager chomps.

Gar again sniffed the ground. "They smell putrid," he insisted.

"All the more for me, then," Gubu happily declared.

Gar, unable to bear the thought of Gubu allocating the entire find to himself, promptly set about munching the berries fallen on his side. "Rancid, yet refreshing!" he admitted amidst zealous gobbles. The two were later spared from worse headaches only by the limited quantity.

"I suppose we should be going now," Gar finally bemoaned. "Which way?"

"There," replied Gubu, "between the two rocks." With considerable effort they aligned themselves, pulling sometimes to the left, sometimes to the right, more or less averaging to a straight path toward the empty space between. Gar found it puzzling, and more than a bit unfair, that the stones on either side kept shifting.

"Perchance, is there only one rock?" Gar demanded upon smacking into a solitary obstacle.

"If not more," Gubu answered, his vision now blurring into three. Eventually they navigated around the unknown number of barriers and proceeded, by fits and starts, to the festival.

∼)(∽

Travelling in the opposite direction, the twins and the Chattiwog had reached the jinjibar tree. "Eminalda!" Fruku cried for the second time that day.

The tiny hostess, now more accustomed to receiving visitors, quickly ascended her beloved ladder. "Land sakes!" she exclaimed. "I sent you off to warn your parents, and instead you return with a feather duster."

"This is our friend, Kiparu," Fruku corrected.

"Oh, beg pardon," Eminalda replied. "I must need new glasses." The shrew squinted through her bifocals, discerning that in fact the plumage belonged to an intact bird.

"He's a screechiwog," Kedra added. "Well, we call him a Chattiwog, actually. And he flies normally, too."

"There, you see," Eminalda replied with delight. "I told you there was such a thing. Years ago, anyway. Though I am 337, give or take, the memory is still as sharp as a tack."

Kiparu took interest in the claim of forward-flying ancestors, but circumstances did not allow him to pursue it further. "Pleased to meet you," he simply offered.

"No doubt you are," answered Eminalda. "And now, concerning me, what do you think of my sun bonnet?"

"It's most becoming," Kiparu responded, taking a cue from Kedra.

"I approve of your friend," Eminalda declared to the twins. "He is well mannered, and that is indeed a rarity these days."

"Look," Fruku said, "I don't want to seem rude, but we are short for time. The Mudupan could be here any moment."

"It won't, though," Eminalda asserted.

"And why not?" wondered Fruku.

"Because," Eminalda explained, "I moved here to be rid of the beast. And if it came here, that would spoil my plan, wouldn't it. So I won't have any talk about The Mudupan coming this way!" The others found the line of thought less than fully persuasive, as their expressions belied. "Then there is the small matter of the knotty jinjibars," Eminalda continued. "The Mudupan can't tolerate the scent. As a top-notch botanist, I can promise you that."

"That leaves only Gronk Narrows," Kedra said. "If we rush, we might arrive just before sunset." A shudder came over her as she considered that very thought.

"Yes, time is of the essence," Eminalda agreed. "We'll go straight away. That is, after I gather a few odds and ends for the battle. Well," she continued, noting the confused stares, "the last thing we want is to fight The Mudupan empty-handed." Kiparu and the twins still were not convinced, but Eminalda had already disappeared. Various rustling sounds came from the hollows. "Take this," she said to whomever could hear before tossing a sack through the hole. Eminalda then pushed her punching bag up the ladder. Fruku could see no value in bringing the oddball, but felt that arguing would be even more pointless. "Right, then," she declared, smacking her little paws together, "away we go!" At that she jumped into Fruku's shirt pocket, which was the perfect size.

Some time later the band of four were nearing Gronk Narrows. "I don't mean to be a wet blanket," said Kiparu, "but do we have a strategy?" From the silence it was clear that none had given much consideration to how, exactly, The Mudupan could be stopped. "Fine," continued the Chattiwog, "let's conduct an inventory."

"An inventory?" Fruku questioned.

"That's right," Kiparu affirmed. "We'll take stock of our assets. That is the one thing we screechiwogs are good at, given the need to keep track of who we've lost on the way. For example: one bird, who can spy from the air. Next?"

"My turn," Kedra said. "One girl who can . . . well, I don't know. I've never done anything like this before."

"No matter," Eminalda assured her. "Are you creative?"

"Well yes, I suppose so."

"Excellent, that might be useful," Kiparu continued. "Now you," he said, gesturing to Fruku.

"And a twin brother who . . ." Fruku also was at a loss.

"Are you brave?" Kiparu prompted.

"I'd like to think so," Fruku answered. "But to be honest, I'm a little afraid."

"Then you are brave, if you can admit that," Kiparu promised. He then turned to Eminalda. "And finally, what is your strength?"

"Let's bash The Mudupan seven ways from Sunday!" shouted the shrew, shaking her fist above the top of Fruku's pocket.

"That's not an asset," Kedra noted.

"Pish-tosh," Eminalda replied. "You know what number concerns me? One, as in one Mudupan down and out for the count."

"And," added Kiparu, returning to the inventory, "one cantankerous pocket shrew, punching far above her weight."

"Highly concentrated vitriol," Eminalda proudly affirmed. "That's what I am!"

"What else?" asked the Chattiwog. "Do we have any tools with us?"

"None, I'm afraid," Fruku answered.

The rider in his pocket was of another view entirely. "Why none indeed!" Eminalda objected.

"What did you take with you from your hole?" inquired Kiparu.

"A wide assortment," Eminalda replied. "A lucky charm, a leather band, pots and pans, a sewing kit . . ."

"With due respect," Kedra interjected, "I don't see how any of that will help us."

"Look," the shrew replied, "I don't know how you pack for danger, but as for me, if a button falls off I certainly want a needle and thread on hand. And you never know when a fire might be useful."

"Do you have matches?" Kedra asked.

"Of course," Eminalda replied. "What good are pots and pans otherwise?"

At that moment an idea started to hatch.

Meanwhile, in a safer spot, the Masters of Ceremonies made their entrance, by zigzags and with considerable ruckus. Even the mayor, who was preoccupied with the final preparations, did not fail to notice that something was amiss.

"You're late!" he admonished. Noticing their lethargic walk and the pinkishness of Gar's nose, scraped and swollen from the collision with an indeterminate number of rocks, the mayor added, "and in a sorry state on top of it. Are you drunk, or simply in a strange mood?"

"Yes," the two heads cheerily confessed at once. The pangs caused by their boisterous reply alerted GubuGar that they might have eaten a few rotten berries too many, and ought to nap away their discomfort. And so the supposed guests of honor quietly slunk away.

"Are you sure this will work?" Kedra whispered. She, Fruku, and Eminalda were huddled behind a dark bend in

Gronk Narrows. Kiparu soared overhead, waiting to signal them at the first sign of The Mudupan.

"Definitely," Eminalda affirmed.

"When do my ideas not work?" Fruku asked.

Kedra grimaced as she thought through the recent cases. "If I'm not mistaken, you also said that before we wound up with slippery floors, a glowing roof . . . ."

"Oh double snap," replied Fruku. "But do we have a choice?"

"Oh triple snap!" said Kedra.

Kiparu banked abruptly, which the others took to mean that he had spotted the beast. They need not have asked the Chattiwog upon his rough landing, for by then they could hear the first echoes of approaching steps. Soon the ground trembled, only slightly at first, but even that was enough to wear on the nerves.

Eminalda sniffed the air. "Foo," she said, "that is one mangy creature!" The twins also caught the first unpleasant wafts, and were none too happy to contend with the odor on top of the other problems. "Luck is on our side," Eminalda assured them. "It's much better to be downwind of the beast than the other way around." The shaking grew in intensity, and with it, the pungent scent. Kedra pinched her nose. Fruku gladly would have followed her lead if he had a free hand.

"Positions, everyone," Eminalda ordered. On her command Kedra started to climb the left bank of the canyon. "Don't miss," Fruku pleaded. Kedra returned an annoyed look before reaching her vantage, from where she could see the letter "X" scrawled near the bottom of the opposite wall. Fruku crouched low to the ground with a matchbox in hand. Kiparu folded his wings into a ball. Next to him, Eminalda jumped up onto an adjacent perch. Each held his or her assigned spot, restraining the urge to run.

Boom. BOOM. BOOM! The narrows shook violently as The Mudupan was nearly upon them. *Why doesn't she give the sign?* Fruku wondered as he looked at Kedra. Finally, she dropped her arm.

"Mudupan!" Eminalda addressed in her most threatening of voices. The beast broke stride to look downward to the left and right. Fruku then struck the match, projecting the shrew's enlarged shadow against the face of the cliff. "You come in expectation of conquest, yet it is *your* day of reckoning!" Disoriented and chagrined, The Mudupan stiffened for battle.

"For the destruction you have caused, for the suffering you have spread," decreed Eminalda, "the earth demands vengeance. Thus shall the very rocks rise against you!" On cue, Kiparu slowly straightened and unfurled his wings, casting a truly apocalyptic profile against the wall. So provoked, the beast was in a thoroughly wild state, and would either flee or attack.

"And as punishment," continued Eminalda, doing her best imitation of a sorceress, "a spell shall be cast upon you. That you may know the fear you have inflicted on others, you will be shrunk to the size of a mouse!" At that Kedra heaved the oddball, scoring a direct hit on the beast's nose. It bent to pick up the bouncing object, rotating it to find a tiny version of itself staring back.

And then something not previously recorded in the annals of Wiggiwump history occurred: The Mudupan was so thoroughly scared out of its wits that it shed its fur. Not simply a little, but entirely, and all at once, and its teeth too for good measure. The creature stood trembling, hairless and thin as if sheered, and puckering. Stripped thus of its cover, the once dreaded Mudupan let out a terrified scream and bounded back to the safety of its lair. All that remained were the pile of reeky fleece, oily fangs, and giant hoof prints, spaced apart four times the usual span.

"And there's plenty more where that came from," yelled Eminalda for good measure. She was still shaking a paw, though by now only at the fading trail of a diminished monster.

$$\sim)(\sim$$

"We've done it!" cried Kedra, rushing to join the others.

"We really have!" Fruku joined in. "We've frightened off The Mudupan."

"Hoorah!" shouted Kiparu.

"No one will ever believe it." Kedra meant, of course, that their heroism was beyond measure. But it was also true, she realized.

Fruku, too, understood that the tale could hardly be recounted, and felt a consequent twinge of sadness. "Unless," he added, referring to Eminalda and Kiparu, "the two of you come with us."

"Yes, come," Kedra agreed. "Let us introduce you to our parents."

Each mulled over the invitation silently. "That's very kind," Kiparu said at last. "But I'm not sure how they will react to a forward-flying Chattiwog."

"Or a pocket shrew," Eminalda concurred.

"Why do you call yourself that?" Kedra wondered.

"Isn't it obvious?" Eminalda wondered. "As you can see for yourself, I fit so nicely into one."

"True," said Fruku. "But all the same, you taught us that courage matters, not size. For scaring off The Mudupan, I think you should be a Lion-Hearted Shrew."

Kedra gently extended the palm of her hand, onto which Eminalda jumped. "Oh, I do like the sound of that!" she declared. "It's even better than Dame Eminalda. My friends will be so impressed." And then, after a pause, she added, "I do still have a few left, actually. Maybe it's high time to find them. Yes, that's a capital idea! They would so enjoy hearing of my latest adventures. Who am I to deprive them of that?"

"What about your home," Fruku asked, "the one The Mudupan destroyed?"

"It will be a good many moons before that sorry excuse for a monster dares to set out into the light again. I'll be safe rebuilding."

"And your tree hole?" Kedra wondered.

"Why, I'll keep it, of course," Eminalda decided. "As my summer home. I always wanted one." The thought clearly pleased her. "Now, if you'll pardon me, I have much work to do."

"I'll be off as well," added Kiparu.

"Where will you go?" Kedra asked.

"I'm not sure," the Chattiwog replied. "To wherever holds the key to mysteries, hopefully."

"Wait," Eminalda interjected. "I have something for you." She asked Fruku to open her sack, into which she leapt. She then emerged with the leather belt, which looked to be a perfect fit for Kiparu. The side pouch was just large enough to store whatever small items might be worth bringing back.

Kiparu was deeply touched by the gesture. "Thank you," he said with earnest surprise. "This is my first gift. And I will be sure to put it to good use." Eminalda fastened the present around Kiparu's neck. Indeed, it fit to a tee.

Kedra felt a mixture of joy and sorrow. "Will we see you again?" she asked.

"Of course," the Chattiwog assured her. "The Glen is a small place. Just waive when you see me in the sky, and if I spot you I'll dip my wing." Kiparu then bowed his head and made his first elegant ascent, into the welcoming heavens.

"You kids should be on your way too," Eminalda advised. "By now your parents will be worried about you. And they should: children ought not to keep such troublesome company."

"But we frightened it away," Fruku replied.

"I was referring to myself!" she said with a mischievous grin. The twins smiled back, lingering only to collect a few strands of Mudupan hair and several fangs for posterity. *Now there go two of the brightest, most alive Wiggiwumps I have ever seen*, Eminalda thought as she watched them bound away. *They will have their ups and downs, to be sure, but sooner or later others will fall in line behind them.*

CHAPTER 9

....

For the Valiant, Triumph

*in which our heroes return unheralded yet content, Harvest Fest
ends on a strange note, and the Sygards look to a bright future*

eanwhile, in the town center, where the smiles
were many and brackawack tea flowed freely, it
seemed there could scarcely be a worry in the
whole of the Glen. Various fire breathers, sword swallowers,
and magicians had dazzled the throngs. The last rays of
the setting sun fell now upon the stages, signaling that the
celebration was nearing its grand finale. In their place, the
fires of flambeaux torches cast dancing shadows throughout
the streets and square.

GubuGar, dressed in what they took to be their
finest, waddled proudly onto the stage, tipping even
more precariously than was their custom. "Ladies and
Gentlemen, your attention, please," Gar requested as the

organizers exchanged confused glances. "As the Masters of Ceremonies, it gives us great pleasure to present the Mayor of Wiggiwump Village." "The honorable Tapron Guggles," Gubu garbled.

"Thank you, GubuGar," replied the mayor, slightly shaken by the unscripted introduction. He then paused briefly while fumbling for his speech. "We here in the Glen are blessed with a life of riches," he began to nods of approval. Gapron proceeded to enumerate the many comforts, from the town planning left by the founders, to science and art, and the literary tradition that linked them to generations past. "And that is why," he suggested, "we have the luxury of charting a new course. As we mark Harvest Fest this year, let us gain a different perspective." A portion of the audience clapped out of politeness, while the rest wisely reserved judgement.

"Join me," he continued, "in a celebration of marching in reverse! And in keeping with the theme of our festival this year, our youth brass band will now close with an original symphony." Noticing the irked stare of Lilliwan he paused uncomfortably, grasping at his tie.

"Anuovwokin," prompted Humberbred, who had shadowed his uncle throughout the day.

"'The Skies,' he continued, "otherwise known as 'A New Way of Walking,' composed and led by our village director, Lilliwan Sygard."

A hush fell over the crowd as Lilliwan lifted her baton. She held it high, freezing for a moment while surveying the audience — *strange, she thought, where are the twins?* — and musicians. By facial expressions and her free hand she then signaled, *Get ready to come in, Oh, do sit up straight,* and *There's no need to be nervous.* A special wink at Rispard meant, *Just wait, your chance will come later.* Gracefully and with perfect timing, Lilliwan drew a triangle in the air. On the second cycle the musicians commenced a spirited waltz, each entering in turn. Their notes mingled in sublime harmony, as if the stick in Lilliwan's hand were a magic wand, drawing from each player a supernatural stream that in turn cast a spell over the listeners.

The band adeptly played the energetic first movement. Lilliwan then lowered her baton to draw them into the plaintive passage to follow. The moment was flawless.

Or nearly so: as the music softened Lilliwan detected the faintest of discords. At first it was barely perceptible, even to the trained ear, yet it was present all the same. Lilliwan scanned the stage to find the source, and then realized that the dissonance was not in the notes carrying upward, but from something already there.

As to *why* the cries came at that moment, discussion long persisted. Some believed that in the blaring of horns the screechiwogs divined kindred spirits and flew to join them. On further reflection others supposed the birds to have nested on Tryg Mountain, whence the panicked retreat of The Mudupan caused their frightened exodus. And a few, the Sygards among them, later took comfort in the thought that the hand of fate occasionally leaves an imprint altogether different.

But *that* it occurred brooked no argument. Lilliwan, hoping that the wedge would pass by harmlessly, signaled, *Play on*. Indeed, the audience might have continued in a swoon had not the lead birds, becoming particularly disoriented, began a rapid descent. The first to strike let out a deafening *bweeet!* that droned out the horns. A second tore the mayor's beloved Harvest Fest banner in half, and a third scored a direct hit into Humberbred, knocking him from the rostrum. Within seconds others collided into the village square, Spiral Tower, and the band shell, some ricocheting from one to the other.

"Don't panic!" entreated the mayor. He was right to plead for calm, of course. Yet, in a moment of agitation, such is the effect of the word *panic* that all else will be ignored. And so the audience went into a frenzy, scattering hither and yon. Only Apseron remained. "Fascinating," he uttered, "there's no rhyme or reason to the formation whatsoever!"

On the band stage only Lilliwan and Rispard, who was under no circumstance prepared to miss his big moment, remained. When a Screechiwog landed with a muffled *thwunk* tail-first into the bell end of his instrument, he might easily have been forgiven for suffering trauma, if not being knocked onto his own haunches. But it takes a healthy set of lungs to blow a bazziba, and Rispard, having a frame to match, felt only a jolt. He calmly let out a blast of his own into the mouthpiece, ejecting the scared intruder. Surprised and no doubt offended, the screechiwog shrieked atrociously before continuing its calamitous journey.

Such was the scene that greeted Kedra and Fruku as they returned from Gronk Narrows. What, exactly, they expected to find, they could not say. A hero's welcome would have befitted them. But as their deed was yet unknown, this ending was not to be. Perhaps they anticipated quietly joining the ranks of celebratory villagers. But in no case could they have imagined finding the town square in a state as if leveled by The Mudupan.

Druzina was the first to intercept them. "Kedra and Fruku," she moaned, as usual using their names disparagingly. "It wouldn't surprise me at all if the two of you had something to do with this mess."

The twins, not in a mood for annoyances, decided to dispatch her without further ado. "Here," Fruku said, handing Druzina a long, pointy fang. "We have a present for you."

"What's this?" Druzina asked, wrinkling her nose. "It's absolutely putrid!"

"Take it," Kedra insisted. "That way you'll be able to recognize the smell of The Mudupan. It likes to eat sweet girls the best!" At that Druzina's precious eyes grew the size of saucers. She ran, screaming all the way back to her room, locking the door and refusing to leave for days.

As they approached the rostrum Kedra and Fruku heard a muffled groan. "That's Humberbred," said Fruku, recognizing the sprawled figure. "Let's help him up."

"Are you alright?" Kedra asked.

"Fine, I think," Humberbred replied, gently touching a bump on his head.

"You're talking normally!" Kedra exclaimed with surprise. For his part, Humberbred had always regarded himself a first-rate orator, and made a remark to that effect. The twins might have dwelt on the matter, but having already witnessed far stranger occurrences that day decided not to pursue it further.

Lilliwan was the first to notice them. "Kids, you're safe," she cried with relief, running to embrace them.

"Yes," Fruku answered, "and you won't believe what we just did!" He desperately wanted to tell of their adventure. But, as Fruku quickly realized, recounting the tale of a Chattiwog, a Lion-Hearted Shrew, and The Mudupan would test the outermost boundaries of imagination, and thus require the right moment. Kedra thought as much and expressed, with a silent glance, *another time.*

"You missed quite a scene," Apseron added, joining them.

"You too," replied Kedra. The twins could not fully suppress satisfied smiles.

Mayor Tuggles, convinced that the danger had passed, emerged from behind the podium. "All clear," he announced. Alas, he did not account for the Omega Screechiwog, which was delayed by a crosswind. But now, making the necessary adjustment, the bird readied his approach. Which shriek was the more ear-splitting, the bleating of the final assailant on flying tail-first into a horrified face, or the cry of the mayor in suffering the indignity of being on the receiving end, was to be long debated in the village.

Countless feathers were still swirling when a solitary bloodshot eye, not yet focusing properly, peered unnoticed above the stage. "Heavens," declared Gubu with alarm, "it's a blizzard!" "What's *hrooooh* that?" yawned Gar. The latter sniffed at the air in disbelief, his large nose vacuuming in fluffs of screechiwog down as it inhaled. He then let out a loud "achoo!" as puffs tickled the underside, taking the sneeze as confirmation of snow. An unbearable shiver then came over GubuGar, who complained that prophets were nowhere welcome in their own lands. And then the self-appointed guardian of Throgwottum Glen slunk back below the stage to curl up, jiparix-like, into a warm ball.

The more reasoned residents of the Glen started to come out of hiding, Vreena among them. "I've never seen the village in such a state. But you kids look none the worse for wear," she continued, noticing the twins' contrasting inner calm.

The children again realized that the full story would need to wait. "I think we are over Wonkus," Kedra explained. Vreena briefly considered confessing her ruse, but then realized there might be such a condition after all. And truly, who is to say there isn't, if only by another name?

～◯◯～

And so the Sygards stood for some time in quiet contemplation. "Isn't the sky breathtaking tonight?" Apseron at last remarked, gazing westward at the fleeting palette of red and orange hues. That such an appreciation came from the scientist among them seemed not at all out of place, and the others nodded in contented agreement. Apseron then looked at the brackawack fields, imagining how a glowing irrigation system might further transform the hill.

Far off on the horizon, a Chattiwog, gaining confidence in his new way of flight, dipped a wing before continuing on to escapades unknown. The eastern winds carried what seemed to be the feint strains of a familiar melody. "Is that 'A Bonny Bright Day in the Glen?'" Lilliwan asked. The twins simply smiled, exchanged a furtive glance, and wondered, silently, what adventures yet lay ahead.

The end.

ABOUT THE AUTHOR

B rian Tremain Gill is an international lawyer by trade, a former quasi diplomat by accident, and a writer by calling. His middle name comes from the children's book by Esther Forbes. He might have lived up to literary expectations sooner if not for a habit of venturing off to faraway lands—although consequently he would have fewer interesting tales to tell.

In 1992, Brian spent the summer in Armenia, where he endured bombardments from neighboring Azerbaijan. Eight years later, he worked in Turkmenistan under constant surveillance. He, his wife, and their first son were in Kyrgyzstan during the coup of 2005, living within yards of a street beset by looters and arsonists. In 2008, his family, now with a second son, managed to be in the middle of both a shelling (Ashkelon, Israel) and war (Tbilisi, Georgia). Brian's professors had emphasized that international law may be practiced from the comfort of an air-conditioned office. Approximately once a month, he regrets not heeding their advice. The rest of the time he feels deeply enriched by his encounters and grateful to have emerged unscathed. Every day he hopes to put his experiences to positive use.

Printed in the United States
By Bookmasters